THE DOPA PROJECT

BY ROBERT RAHULA

ALSO BY ROBERT RAHULA

NOVELS:
Messieurs
Panamaniac
Island of Misfits
Day Another Paradise In
One Last Fling
Bathhouse Stories
Conversation in a Belgian Bar
All the Yage in Reno
Exigent Circumstances
Uninvited Guest
A Modest Summation of Things
To Die in Toledo
The Treasure of the Gran Ventura
Inauthenticity
Weightless
The Erikschitz Principle

SHORT STORIES:
Horror Stories for Children
Behind the Pearly Gates

POETRY:
Trigger Points
Dentro Del Corazón Bloqueada
Camino
Migration
I Sing the Body Politic
Wonderland
From Whose Bourn
Poemas Españoles
Expat Poems
Old Dogs New Poems

ANTHOLOGIES:
Half Life
The Essential Dan Landes
50 Years Down the Drain

THE DOPA PROJECT

© 2024 by Robert Rahula
First Printing 2025

All rights reserved. This book or any portion thereof may not be reproduced or used in any manner whatsoever without the express written permission of the author except for the use of brief quotations in a book review.

www.robertrahula.com

This is a work of fiction. Characters, organizations, businesses, products, locales, and events portrayed in this book either are products of the author's imagination or are used fictitiously.

ISBN 979-8-9897238-3-6

Alma-gator Press
Barcelona • Madrid • La Chorrera

PROLOGUE

Reno, Nevada

Darryl had been losing at the craps table all night long. He was tired and irritable. Despite the casino's air conditioning system, his eyes burned from all the cigarette smoke. He got up, walked over to the ATM machine and pulled the last of his paycheck out of his checking account. He came back to the table, bought some chips, and bet $25 on the pass line. The shooter rolled. The point was ten. Darryl could work with that. He took $25 odds on the ten. Then he placed $440 on the four inside numbers: five, six, eight, and nine. He told himself that he just needed to hit the inside numbers a couple of times, and then he would quit. But when he hit the five, he decided to full press it. Then he hit the five again, and he decided to full press it again. Then, miraculously, he hit the five a third time, and so he full pressed it a third time. Now he had $1770 in bets on the table. This could be it, he thought. His luck was finally turning—he could feel it. He only had to hit the inside numbers three more times and he'd have some real cash. The shooter picked up the dice, gave them a quick shake, and tossed them into the air.

* * *

San Francisco, California

Steven walked out of rehab with his thirty-day graduation papers neatly folded in his pocket. His uncle had given him some money as a graduation present. Steven took the bus down to Mason Street. It took him about ten minutes to find Doodle, who sold him one pill of Pink Ivory for three dollars. Doodle told him it was Oxy, but Steven knew it was probably fentanyl, which was fine with him.

Later, after Steven had passed out in the alley, Doodle went through his pockets and took the rest of the money his uncle had given him.

* * *

Fort Lauderdale, Florida

Richard and Michael were soaking together in the big hot tub at the bathhouse and chatting when Richard announced, "I've been toying with the idea of going to Thailand in December or January."

"Really? Thailand? That's pretty far away," said Michael.

"Yeah, but I need something big to look forward to. I hate the holidays when all the snowbirds come down here. I thought it would be fun to go somewhere exotic, see the elephants, eat authentic Thai food, visit the temples."

Michael gave Richard a knowing look and said, "I know you, my friend. You're thinking about going to Bangkok, aren't you? And it's not for the food or the elephants or the temples. It's for the ladyboys!"

Richard just smiled.

* * *

Charlotte, North Carolina

    Madeline used to be embarrassed to go down to the local 7-11 to buy her lottery tickets, but a friend from the Bingo Hall showed her how to buy them online. Madeline had taken a free computer course at the community center last year to learn how to email her grandchildren, so she caught on to the lottery app pretty quickly. She started playing the Powerball and the Mega Millions online, but the daily Lotto was her favorite. She opened a new credit card without telling her husband. Luckily, he didn't know a thing about computers, but still, Madeline had to take great effort to hide her gambling from him.

* * *

Tulsa, Oklahoma

    Martin sat at the bar and finished his first whisky over ice. "Now that's a gentleman's drink," he thought to himself as he signaled the bartender for another. For a moment, the image of Susan sitting at home with the kids flashed through his mind, but he pushed it down. "A man needs a break every once in a while," he told himself as the bartender brought him another whisky. It had been a tough day at work. He needed to relax a bit before going home. "Just one more," he told himself.

* * *

CHAPTER ONE

Alexandria, Virginia

Ben Wozniak first heard about the drug Dopa from his girlfriend, Sarah Mihelich. Sarah had a PhD in Behavioral Neurobiology. She worked as a research director in neurology at the National Institute of Health. Her job required her to keep up to date with all sorts of different scientific news. Thus, she often spent her spare time perusing scientific journals online, even on her days off.

It irritated Ben that she spent so much of her free time staring at a laptop screen. But he really wasn't in a position to complain about it, since he did the exact same thing. Ben was an independent investigative reporter. He had had articles published by ProPublica and was credited as a researcher and writer on several Frontline pieces. He was always on the lookout for a new story.

Ben and Sarah had been dating for almost three years. Their relationship had that interesting but annoying dynamic that often occurs when two successful people pair up. It was almost as if the success and accolades that they each had in their separate jobs didn't carry over into the relationship. Instead, the relationship became the testing ground for all the insecurities they had about their respective professions. Their therapist had pointed out to them how the need to prove their intelligence to each other created a certain unhealthy competition to their communication. But Ben and Sarah were working on this. They were both committed to their relationship. They were very compatible.

They enjoyed spending time with each other. And, on some level, they each recognized that neither one of them would ever find a better partner. Some people call this love.

And so it was, that on a particular Sunday afternoon in Alexandria, Virginia, Sarah was sitting on the couch with her laptop in Ben's apartment, scanning through articles from different scientific journals, while Ben was sitting at a small table by the front bay window, also scrolling through his laptop.

"Huh... Dr. Gaye has disappeared," Sarah muttered half-aloud to herself.

Ben looked up briefly before returning his gaze to his computer screen, but he said, "Oh yeah? Who's that?"

"He's the doctor who invented Dopa," she responded.

"What's Dopa?" asked Ben.

"It's a new drug to treat addiction. It showed great promise in the early trials. Pfizer and Novo Nordisk were getting ready to put some serious money into it. Now Dr. Gaye, who developed the drug, has vanished."

Ben was more interested now. "Was there some kind of fraud going on?" he asked.

"No, it doesn't appear so. No one had invested any money beyond the preliminary clinical trials, which were funded by Stanford. The trials are in the process of peer-review. Dr. Gaye should have been sitting on top of the world. He was the sole holder of the patent."

"And this is a treatment for drug addiction?" Ben asked.

"Well, more than that," Sarah said. "That's what makes Dopa so promising. It seems to be effective against a variety of addictions: drugs, alcohol, smoking, gambling—any kind of compulsive addictive behavior. Most of the current medications only target a single addiction. For example, naltrexone treats opioid addiction by blocking the receptors in the brain so you don't get high. But naltrexone only works well against opioids; it's not as effective against amphetamines or cocaine. Kinda like how those nicotine patches only work against cigarette addiction. Dopa is different. It's supposed to block the part of the brain that engages in compulsive addictive behavior, regardless of what the addiction is."

"Interesting," said Ben. "So what happened to this guy?"

"Well, he's just disappeared, vanished from his home in Napa, California. His daughter had called the police for a welfare check because she hadn't heard from him for a couple of days. When the police got there, they found the house in complete disarray, like it had been burglarized, and Dr. Gaye was gone. It's a mystery."

"I like mysteries," Ben said, and closed his laptop and came over to sit down next to Sarah on the couch.

"What's his full name?" he asked.

"Dr. Disraeli Gaye," she said.

"Immigrant?"

"Nope. Born in New Jersey. Here's his bio," and Sarah hit a few keys and turned her laptop so that Ben could see it.

"Fifty-eight years old, MD, PhD, professor at Stanford... owns several medical patents on different drugs..." Ben read aloud. "And his photograph certainly looks professorial ... Can you show me the article about his disappearance?"

Sarah typed on her laptop for a moment until the article came up on the screen. Then she handed the laptop to Ben.

Ben read through it and then handed the laptop back to Sarah. Now he was definitely interested. "Tell me more about this drug Dopa," he said. "Like, why is it called Dopa?"

"That was Dr. Gaye's suggested brand name for it when he pitched it to investors. But I think people call it that because the real name is complicated. It's a genetically modified drug that combines levodopa, which is the body's precursor to dopamine, and gamma-aminobutryic acid, which is..."

"No, no," protested Ben. "Just tell me about what it does. Tell me in simple terms."

"Okay. Well, the theory has been around for a while... in fact, it's accepted science now, that different parts of the brain work together to handle different aspects of addiction... that addiction is like... well, it's like an assembly line in the brain that is coordinated by different managers who live in different parts of the brain. For example, if you have back pain, the nerves in your back send a message to your brain saying that your back hurts, and your brain releases these natural opioids called endorphins to counteract the pain. And those endorphins work by binding with receptors in the brain and spinal cord to reduce the pain. They *mollify* the pain; they don't eliminate it, because your brain still needs to know what's going on with your back, but they reduce it; they manage it. But, if you take an opioid medication, that medication *completely* blocks those same receptors, so you don't feel *any* pain. And if that's *all* that opioids did—if they just *blocked* pain—we wouldn't have addiction, but opioids do a hell of a lot more. They also seep into the mid-part of the brain, the area that controls euphoria and pleasure, and they bind with all *those* receptors, and then that part of the brain starts releasing huge amounts of dopamine, and suddenly, you feel *great!* Then, the prefrontal cortex of the brain, which is where learning happens, gets involved and immediately figures out that the opioid drug is making you feel great. Then the prefrontal cortex coordinates with the thalamus and basal ganglia in the central part of the brain to figure out how to repeat this behavior. And the reason they want to repeat the behavior is that the amount of dopamine that is released is so overwhelming, that when it's turned off, the brain panics. There are a number of studies that show how the actual physical structure of the brain changes to start creating the obsession to repeat the euphoric experience. That's why addiction has been classified as a *brain disease*. Opioids are so powerful that they change the brain. The addict really has no control over their behavior... You follow me so far?"

Ben nodded his head and said, "I think so."

Sarah continued. "Anyway, the important thing to understand is that different drugs trigger the release of dopamine in different areas of the brain. Opioids trigger dopamine in one area, but amphetamine triggers dopamine in another area. And because different treatment medicines affect different nerve receptors, you need a different medication to counteract each addictive drug. But what Dr. Gaye discovered was that no matter what addictive drug was involved, it always affected the *same* area of the prefrontal cortex. That is, regardless of the addiction, the part of the brain that tries to figure out how to repeat the behavior is the same. And so he developed Dopa to specifically target this part of the prefrontal cortex. Supposedly, it blocks the brain from creating a compulsive repetitive behavior to feed the addiction. It blocks the panic. The addict will still get high if he takes opioids, but he doesn't have the *compulsion* to get high anymore. Dopa restores rational thinking. It allows the addict to exert control over the addiction. And what makes Dopa such a potential break-through, is that it seems to also work on addictions like gambling and sex addiction. Those addictions are difficult to treat because there is no external chemical trigger for them. The gambler isn't taking a drug; he's just hooked on the dopamine release that the anticipation of winning gives him. But what Dr. Gaye discovered is that the prefrontal cortex process is exactly the same for the gambling addict as for the opioid addict. Compulsive addiction is compulsive addiction, no matter what you're addicted to."

Ben leaned back on the couch, folded his hands on the top of his head, and just stared off into space. "Wow," he said. "That all kind of makes sense. And if this Dopa treatment really worked, it would be worth millions."

"Billions," Sarah said, "maybe trillions. It would completely change the treatment for addiction. That's what makes it so weird that Dr. Gaye has just vanished."

Ben sat quiet for a full minute, thinking deeply. Finally he said, "Honey, can you forward all the articles on this doctor and Dopa to me? I need to call my editor."

CHAPTER TWO

Villa Rosario, Panama

Police Chief José Fernando had a problem. He was sitting in his office in the police station in Villa Rosario, turning the problem over in his mind. José Fernando (or as he was more commonly called, don Fernando), was the police chief of the small town of Villa Rosario. He had been the police chief for as long as anyone could remember. Over the years, he had seen the wide variety of difficult situations—both criminal and non-criminal—that people could get themselves into. But this time, he was concerned. He wasn't sure what to do. And one thing about don Fernando: he did not want to make a mistake. Finally, he picked up the phone and dialed his friend, Dan Landes.

Dan answered the phone.

"Hola, Dani. I was hoping I could find you. Are you at home?"

"Yup. Just got up from a nap. What's up?"

"Well, Dani. I need some advice. I have one of your countrymen in custody, and I'm not exactly sure what to do with him."

"Oh? What did he do?" Dan asked.

"Well, he hasn't done anything yet... but I am concerned for his safety. I think he is a little loco. I have asked for a doctor to come over from La Chorrera to evaluate him. But I was wondering if you could come by and talk to him."

"Me? Why me?"

"Well, he is a gringo. You are a gringo. I thought maybe you could talk with him and help me to understand what he is saying. He talks in—how do you say? He talks in circles. He doesn't make any sense, at least not to me."

"I'm not a psychologist, don Fernando," Dan protested.

"Yes, I know. But maybe this gringo will feel more comfortable talking to you, you know, gringo to gringo. I would be grateful, Dani, if you could do me just this one little favor."

Dan sighed. Whenever don Fernando asked for 'just one little favor,' Dan knew it was important. "Is this guy in your holding cell at the station?" Dan asked.

"Sí, Dani. I did not know where else to put him."

"Okay, don Fernando, give me about fifteen minutes to get organized, and I'll be over."

Dan finished off the half-cup of cold coffee that was left over from the morning, brushed his teeth, and headed down to the police station. Villa Rosario was not a large town, and everything within the town's borders was within walking distance. That was one of the things Dan liked about the town when he moved there from the States some fifteen years ago. That, plus the fact that there weren't many gringos living there. He didn't like the US culture he had left behind, and on the rare occasion when he met a wannabe-expat from the States, he usually found them to be opinionated, entitled, and obnoxious. So the idea of interviewing some fucked-up gringo in the holding cell of the Villa Rosario jail did not appeal to Dan at all. But don Fernando was his best friend, and he couldn't turn him down when he asked for just one little favor.

Dan walked the ten-minute walk across town, past the old Catholic church at the center of town, and through the large Parque Central with its tall palm trees that shaded the walkways and the many concrete benches. The town of Villa Rosario, like most Panamanian towns, was dry, dusty, and brown during the dry season, but the Parque Central was always a green oasis. It was constantly watered and maintained by a crew of groundskeepers who kept it pristine and beautiful. People called it the crown jewel of the town. The fact was, it was the only jewel of the town.

The police station stood on the opposite corner of the park. It was a large building length-wise, but only one story tall and thus, not very imposing. Dan stepped inside, nodded at the desk sergeant, and made his way back to don Fernando's office.

"Ah, Dani. Come in, come in. I just made some fresh coffee."

"Thanks, but I'm good. What's going on?" Dan said as he sat down in the large chair across from don Fernando's desk.

"We picked up this gringo this morning. He was very disoriented, very excited, just wandering through the streets talking to himself very loudly. We found a hotel key in his pocket. Evidently, he has been staying in the Las Palmas Hotel over in La Chorrera. We have no idea how he got to Villa Rosario. The officer who found him thought he had taken some drugs, you know, that made him act crazy."

"Okay," said Dan. "So why not just transport him to the Solano Hospital in La Chorrera? If he's taken some drug, he needs to be seen by a doctor."

"I agree," don Fernando said. "And that was our first plan. But when we told this gringo that, he became very upset and started shouting. He does not want to go back to La Chorrera. He says someone is trying to kill him there."

"Ah, so he's paranoid. Well, that could be the effect of some drug."

"Yes, we thought that, too. But when the La Chorrera police went to his hotel room, they found that the sliding glass door to his balcony had three bullet holes in it. And they found the bullet slugs imbedded in the wall inside the room. It looked like someone had tried to shoot at him from the street."

Dan sat back and crossed his arms. This was something totally different. "Really?" he said. "Did they interview the hotel staff?"

"Yes. The front desk manager said he heard something, but thought it was a car backfiring. But then he saw the gringo leave the hotel in a hurry."

"Okay," said Dan. "What's this guy's name?"

"James Peterson," said don Fernando as he handed Dan a passport.

Dan opened the passport and looked at the photograph of a middle-aged man with gray hair. He flipped through the pages. This was a newly issued US passport. There was only one country's stamp in it, and that was Panama's. Dan went back to the first page and looked at the hologram image on the page. He held the passport up to the light and looked at the colors in the hologram. He ran his finger over the photograph and then examined several of the blank pages.

Then he asked don Fernando, "Do you have a magnifying glass?

Don Fernando rummaged through his desk drawer until he found a large magnifying glass, and handed it to Dan. Dan held it over one of the blank pages and leaned his head in just a few inches above the glass, looking at something on the page.

"I don't know who your Mr. Peterson is," Dan said, "but this passport is a counterfeit."

"Really? How do you know, Dani?"

Dan stood up and walked around don Fernando's desk, and placed the passport down on the desk, holding it open to a blank page with his left hand.

"You see, we're on page seventeen of the passport here..."

Dan handed the magnifying glass to don Fernando, then pointed to a tiny line on the page and said, "Now, look at this line under the magnifying glass. See if you can read it."

"Read it?" don Fernando asked, looking confused. But he held the glass over the line until the tiny words "visa page 17" appeared in focus.

"See how blurry the letters are? They should be crisp and exact. US passports have these tiny words printed on every page. They're printed with special equipment on real passports. It's called *microtext*. They should be high resolution, very distinct—not fuzzy and irregular, like this passport. Counterfeiters simply cannot duplicate such tiny words with any precision."

"Well, I'll be damned," don Fernando said.

"It's a pretty good counterfeit." Dan said. "If the microchip that is imbedded in this passport was programmed correctly, it would fool most immigration officers."

Don Fernando shook his head. "I thought I just had a problem with a crazy gringo. Now I have a problem with a crazy *illegal* gringo," he muttered.

"Whom someone took a shot at," added Dan.

"Yes, so it appears."

"So tell me, what was he saying that was so crazy? Dan asked.

"Oh, Dani, he made no sense at all. I couldn't understand many of the words he was using. They were from a foreign language. But he kept repeating them over and over. I think he is crazy."

"But he understood you when you said you were going to take him back to La Chorrera?"

"Oh, yes, he was quite adamant that he was not safe there."

"So he's not out of touch with reality. Is he in any way violent?" Dan asked.

"No, occasionally he makes loud outbursts, but no violent movements."

"Well, okay," said Dan, "let's go chat with him."

"I'll have him brought to the interview room."

"No, let's not do that," suggested Dan. "That might frighten him. Let's just go back and visit him in the cell." Then Dan picked up the passport and said to don Fernando, "May I borrow this? I may want to use it."

Don Fernando nodded, and Dan stuck the passport in his shirt pocket. The two men walked back to the holding cell area of the Villa Rosario police station.

The holding cells were just that: cells where arrestees were held until they could be transported elsewhere. As mentioned, Villa Rosario was a small town, too small to have its own court system. Anyone arrested inside the town limits had to be transported to the neighboring city of La Chorrera to face charges. The police station had two regular holding cells, each with a sink and an exposed toilet with no privacy, and two single beds where arrestees could sit or lie down. These two holding cells were as basic and stark as one might expect in a foreign police station. But the station also had a third, larger cell, with a separate shower and bathroom, a single full-size bed with a more comfortable mattress, and a comfortable chair for sitting. Don Fernando had added this cell years ago during a remodeling of the station. Prisoners who had money could pay a daily fee to be housed in this cell. It was a way for the police station to earn a little extra cash. Even though the so-called Mr. Peterson did not have any cash on him when he was arrested, he was placed in this larger cell, because he was a gringo.

And on this particular day, Mr. Peterson was the only guest in the holding cells. He was lying down on his bed talking quietly to himself as Dan and don Fernando approached, and he continued to lie there, mumble and just stare at the ceiling as the guard opened the cell and let the two men in.

Dan sat in the chair facing Mr. Peterson while don Fernando stood.

"Hey, buddy," Dan said in a loud voice. "Sit up so we can talk."

Mr. Peterson shook his head as if waking up, and appeared to notice Dan and don Fernando for the first time. He looked around the cell, then slowly sat up, and looked at Dan.

"The problem," he said softly, "is in the pathways for the catecholamines and trace amines. I don't know why I didn't see it before. The tyramines are reverting to phenethylamines. I'm such an idiot. The balance is in the imbalance, not the other way around."

Dan looked at don Fernando. Don Fernando just shrugged as if to say, "See what I mean?"

Dan turned back to Mr. Peterson. "Well, let's start with introductions, shall we? My name is Dan Landes. What's yours?"

"The problem is in the phenethylamines. I have to reverse the reversal," Mr. Peterson muttered.

"Hey buddy," Dan said sternly. "What's your name?"

Mr. Peterson looked up. He squinched his face, trying to think. Then he said, "Peterson," and looked away.

"Liar liar, pants on fire," Dan said in a mocking tone. He pulled the passport out of his shirt pocket, opened it up to the photo page, held it out for Mr. Peterson to see, and said, "I know this is a fake passport. We're not stupid. What's your real name?"

Mr. Peterson squinted at the passport and then at Dan, but said nothing.

"Look buddy," Dan said. "We can take you back to La Chorrera and just drop you off at your hotel. Just drop you off in the middle of the street for everyone to see."

Suddenly Mr. Peterson was animated. "No, no, the Synoids are trying to kill me!"

Dan leaned forward and said, "Yes, I know. They're trying to kill you. And, as a fellow American, I'm trying to fucking help you. But I can't help you if you play games with me. We know this is a counterfeit passport. What is your real name?"

Mr. Peterson looked desperate. His eyes darted left and right.

"If I tell you, you'll protect me from the Synoids?" he asked.

"We'll protect you. You have my word," Dan said.

"You promise?"

"I promise," Dan said.

Mr. Peterson lowered his head and said, "Gaye. Disraeli Gaye."

CHAPTER THREE: INTERLUDE

Reno, Nevada

Darryl sat at the craps table and watched as the stickman swept away the last of his chips. His entire paycheck was gone. He had even taken a cash advance from his only working credit card. He was out of money. He finished his drink, stood up, and stumbled away from the table without looking at the dealers. He felt numb.

* * *

San Francisco, California

Steven woke up in the alley. His head hurt horribly. He ached all over. He reached for his wallet. It was gone. He knew Doodle had robbed him. He tried to stand up, but couldn't. He wondered if rehab would take him back. He had no other place to go.

* * *

Fort Lauderdale, Florida

Michael was still questioning Richard about his plans to visit Thailand.

"Ricky, that's a long way to go just for some ladyboys. There are plenty of nice transwomen in Miami, only thirty minutes away. Why not go there and save your money?"

"I can't help myself, Michael. The Thai ladyboys are just so beautiful. And there's so many of them. Hundreds to choose from. I'll be swimming in ladyboys every day."

"How long is the flight?"

"About twenty-two hours."

"My friend, you are crazy."

* * *

Charlotte, North Carolina

Madeline had maxed out her credit card playing the online lottery games. She opened a new credit card, still without telling her husband. If she could just win even a small jackpot, she could pay off both cards, and her husband would never be the wiser.

* * *

Tulsa, Oklahoma

The bartender came over to Martin and said, "You've probably had enough for tonight, doncha think, Marty?"

Martin nodded. "Yeah," was all he could say.

"How are you getting home?"

Martin held up his keys.

"I don't think you should drive, Marty," the bartender said. "Why don't I call you a cab?"

"Nah, I'll be okay," Martin said and stood up.

* * *

CHAPTER FOUR

Alexandria, Virginia

Ben always had a good nose for a story. His editors at ProPublica knew that. Even though they had some reservations about the story of Dr. Gaye and Dopa, they gave him a budget to start working on it. Their specific reservation was that they wouldn't know in advance where the story was going until the reason for Dr. Gaye's disappearance was discovered. Ben agreed, but argued that the development of the Dopa medicine by itself was worthy of a story. His editors had to agree with that.

With an approved budget, Ben began to compile a list of witnesses to interview. He debated what angle to take. Should he highlight the medical breakthrough? That would mean he would have to start with interviewing the people at the lab at Stanford, which meant that he would have to find out who they were. Or should he focus on the business angle? Sarah had said that Pfizer and Novo Nordisk were getting ready to invest in Dopa. Ben figured that if those companies were reaching for their wallets, it meant that at least a dozen hedge funds would also be licking their lips at the chance to invest. Ben knew a few investors at a couple of funds. It would be a shot in the dark, but maybe he could call them and make some discrete inquiries. Or maybe he should start with the crime scene, and interview the police who had first gone to Dr. Gaye's house.

Finally, Ben decided to start with Dr. Gaye's daughter. It was the obvious choice because it was the easiest, since one of the articles that Sarah had given him had the daughter's name: Lenore Gaye.

It didn't take Ben long to track down Lenore Gaye's address. The internet had everyone's information if you knew where to look. But he didn't email her. He sent her a letter, on ProPublica stationary, through the US Postal Service. The internet had become so polluted with scammers that everyone immediately distrusted an email from a stranger. But a letter, on letterhead, typed out and signed—that was something different. As old-fashioned as it was, people still trusted letters they got in the mail. And so Ben sent Lenore Gaye a letter, introducing himself and explaining that ProPublica was considering doing a piece on Dr. Gaye, and asking if he could interview her. Of course, Ben included his email address for her response. And then he waited. Letters were more effective for getting access to people, but they were slower. He knew it would take a few days for Lenore Gaye to respond, if she responded at all.

While Ben waited, Sarah sent him endless scientific articles on addiction. He found them difficult to read. Not only were the articles full of medical jargon, but the topic itself was complicated. Nonetheless, he forced himself to slog through them, and they all seemed to confirm what Sarah had initially told him: that the prerequisite for drug addiction was the sudden massive release of dopamine in the brain. Drugs that only triggered small amounts of dopamine, like psychedelics, weren't medically addictive; but drugs that triggered large releases of dopamine were. The only exception were drugs that had ongoing delivery systems: drugs that were consumed in small but consistent doses— like coffee, cigarettes, and alcohol. They did not trigger large releases of dopamine, but they allowed dopamine to build up in the brain over time, eventually achieving the same dopamine saturation effect... and addiction.

And the trigger didn't even have to be a drug. Gambling addicts and sex addicts had the same altered brain chemistry as drug addicts. Ben read several studies where gambling addicts were placed in an MRI machine and allowed to gamble online while the MRI recorded the dopamine surges in their brains. Their MRI readings were identical to drug addicts who were placed in MRIs and allowed to take drugs. The gamblers didn't even have to win. Evidently, the anticipation of winning a huge jackpot was enough to trigger a large dopamine release.

And sex, of course, was very addictive. Orgasms triggered large spikes in dopamine, and then the body naturally tried to reset for more orgasms. That made sense to Ben. The survival of the human race depended on continual sexual activity, so the sex/dopamine connection seemed to be programmed into the human brain. But there was very little research on *why* some people became sexual addicts while others didn't. Ben assumed it was simply a matter of social pressure, upbringing, and legal restrictions.

But while dopamine was the starting point for any addiction, after that, it got complicated, especially when it came to medical treatment. Ben couldn't find any agreement among practitioners about which medicines were best for treating drug addiction. Some rehab centers prescribed drugs that blocked dopamine release, while others used medicines that increased dopamine. But it was clear that whatever prescription was used depended on what type of drug the patient said they were addicted to. Methadone or naltrexone were used to treat opioid addiction; Campral was used to treat alcohol addiction; and Ritalin was used to treat amphetamine addiction. But these traditional medical treatments, even when combined with therapy, only had a thirty percent success rate. That was because of the Addiction Replacement or Switch phenomenon. As soon as doctors were able to stop a patient's addiction to one drug, the patient would simply—and surreptitiously—switch to another illicit drug. If opioids failed to get a patient high because his receptors were blocked by medication, the patient would seek out whatever other drug was available to achieve a similar dopamine release. Opioid addicts would switch to amphetamine; alcoholics would switch to opioids; and speed freaks would switch to fentanyl; whatever was available. As one researcher put it when discussing the Switch phenomenon, the addiction was to dopamine, rather than a specific drug of choice.

To Ben's way of thinking, this all supported what Sarah had told him about Dr. Gaye's treatment theory—that the way to treat addiction was to block the *compulsion* to get high rather than the *effect* of getting high. The more Ben read, the more interested he became in Dr. Gaye's drug. But he couldn't find any articles on how Dopa exactly worked. The clinical trials at Stanford had been carefully designed, using double-blind protocol and large groups of subjects, and the peer-review analysis was positive. But Stanford had yet to release a detailed medical explanation of how Dopa blocked the compulsion to repeat the behavior that resulted in dopamine release.

Ben was talking to Sarah about this.

"I hadn't realized that addiction was so complex," he said.

"Addiction isn't complex," Sarah corrected him, "it's the brain that's complex. Addiction doesn't exist without the brain."

"But how come only human brains? Other animals don't have addictions."

"Oh, they would if they could," Sarah said. "You can easily get rats addicted to cocaine—just make it available to them! Give a rat a choice between a bottle of pure water and another bottle laced with cocaine, and the rats will suck on the cocaine bottle all day long. What humans have that other animals don't have is that we have the ability to *manufacture* addictive substances. Monkeys have to wait until they find spoiled fruit on the ground that has fermented before they can get drunk. But we humans have billion-dollar industries devoted to fermenting wine."

"That's true," Ben said.

"Do you know the story of how coffee was discovered?" Sarah asked.

"No."

"Well, the story is that around 800 AD, a goat herder in Ethiopia noticed that when his goats ate the berries of a certain plant, they had extra energy and wouldn't sleep. So he took the berries to a local monastery, and the monks figured out how to brew the berries into a drink. Those berries were coffee beans, and the drinking of coffee spread from Ethiopia like wildfire all over the world. That's the difference between humans and goats—we build the infrastructure to harvest, roast, package, and ship coffee. We organize and distribute our addictions."

"I have to have my coffee," Ben admitted.

"That's because it's so addictive," Sarah countered. "People certainly don't drink it for its taste."

"No, I like the taste of coffee," Ben protested.

"You like it because it's addictive. I dare you to drink decaf for a week," Sarah responded. "It's like cigarettes—the world's most disgusting addiction. You take the nicotine out of cigarettes, and *nobody* would smoke them. Smokers convince themselves they like the smell or taste of cigarettes only because they're addicted to them. All addicts become delusional about the drug they are addicted to. Gamblers romanticize casinos; junkies carry their needles in fancy leather pouches; crack addicts fetishize their little glass pipes; drinkers have their favorite cocktails, and cigarette smokers all pose like they're the Marlboro Man. It's pure delusion!"

"You seem kind of angry about addiction," Ben said.

Sarah frowned and took a breath. "Yeah, sorry, Ben. I get worked up. My dad was an addict, you know. I watched it destroy his life. I didn't mean to rant. It just makes me so mad how society makes it so easy to be an addict, how it glorifies and monetizes drinking, gambling, and drug use; and then just abandons people once they get hooked."

"Sorry," Ben said. "I forgot about your dad. I shouldn't have brought the topic up. It's just that this project is kind of overwhelming to me."

"No, no. I want you to ask me about it. I was excited when you got this project approved. I think the reason I went into neuroscience was because of my dad's suicide... because I wanted to understand. So it helps if we talk about it."

Ben took her hand. "Are you sure?"

"Yeah, I'll try to keep my ranting under control."

"Okay. Well, just a few more questions. I'm just trying to understand why the human brain is so susceptible to addiction. I read how some people become hooked on a drug after only trying it one time. I don't understand that. I mean... one time? I thought that the human brain was the most highly evolved organ that nature has ever created. Why didn't we evolve defenses against addiction?"

Sarah paused. "Well, I don't think it's accurate to call the human brain the most highly evolved organ ever created. I think it's more accurate to say that the human brain is the most *complicated* organ that has ever evolved. The difference is this: To say that something is highly evolved implies that it's efficient, that it's streamlined, that it's nimble and adaptive. That's not our brains. Our brains are more like huge, sprawling governmental bureaucracies that have evolved *without regard* to overall efficiency. The brain has millions of different departments, and each department handles *one* task, and it communicates with only a few other departments. It works, but it works the same way a robot works: so long as it's repeating the same function over and over, it operates efficiently. It's only good at repetitive behaviors. But throw it a new problem, and it grinds to a halt. That's why it's so hard to recover from a brain injury—the other departments can't handle the extra workload when one department is out sick. Remember, the prefrontal cortex, which *tries* to coordinate the brain, came along very late in our evolution.

"But, to answer your question about why some people can become hooked after only trying a drug one time, science doesn't quite understand it. But I can tell you the current theory, and it ties into Dr. Gaye's Dopa medication. There's a part of the brain called the dorsolateral prefrontal cortex..."

"Whoa, that's a mouthful," said Ben. "Remember, I'm not a scientist. Keep it simple for me."

Sarah laughed. "Okay. Let's call it the dlPFC, because that's actually the abbreviation for it. The dlPFC is the part of the brain that has to do with self-control, with discipline, with the ability to say no. But this part of the brain doesn't really develop until you're an adult. The neurons start forming during adolescence, but they don't finish connecting until you're past your mid-twenties. So the younger someone is when they start using drugs, the more likely it is they will become addicted. Their dlPFC isn't developed. They simply don't have the brains to say no.

"But even some older people might have an underdeveloped dlPFC, and thus be more suspectable to addiction. Like any other skill or muscle, self-discipline only develops by repeated practice. Someone who grows up in an environment where they never have to exert self-control usually has an underdeveloped dlPFC. And you can measure this on an MRI. Those people would become addicted the first time they tried a drug and experienced that massive dopamine release. At least, that's the current theory as to why some people get hooked so easily and other people can try a drug once and not use it again."

"Yet, some people are able to overcome addiction," Ben said. "How are they able to do it?"

A look of sadness came over Sarah's face. "I don't know," she said. "It seems so random why some people succeed and others fail. My dad went to rehab five times! It just never took. He'd be fine for months, sometimes years, but then he'd disappear..."

Her voice trailed off. Then she composed herself. "I read a theory recently that said that the people who successfully overcome addiction do so by *replacing* one dopamine release with another. They *exchange* an unhealthy addiction with a healthy addiction. For example, MRIs can measure the amount of dopamine that is released when someone praises you. If you build a peer support group around you that continually praises you for *not* drinking, that praise and adulation—*in itself*—triggers a huge release of dopamine. It's well known that the most successful graduates of AA programs are those people who become AA counselors themselves. They put themselves in positions where their brains are going to get daily dopamine jolts from helping other people not drink or drug.

"Some studies show that recovering addicts who take up serious exercise, like marathon running or weight-lifting, have a higher success rate in staying sober. Again, that's because those activities release large amounts of dopamine. And there's a rehab center in England that seems to be having some success teaching patients to meditate every day, which is an activity that releases dopamine.

"My dad had a friend in one of his rehab groups that took up painting. He was quite good at it. And his paintings sold. And after he graduated from rehab, he developed a nice career as a painter. He got kind of famous. He never went back to drugs because he found an alternative reward system, which was the money and praise he got from painting.

"There's not much research on this theory, but it makes sense to me. And it's why I was a little skeptical of Dr. Gaye's approach when I first read about it. Because I can't see where the dopamine replacement is, so I'm still not sure that Dopa is the total answer. I was wanting to see how his patients did after five years of sobriety, whether they could even make it five years... But now that he's disappeared, well, who knows what will happen with Dopa?"

"He didn't license it out to anyone to continue his research?" Ben asked.

"No. Evidently, he was a control-freak... which kind of doesn't surprise me," Sarah said. "Stanford is trying to put together a team to decide how to proceed, but basically, everyone is just waiting until he shows up."

"According to the last news reports I read," Ben said, "the police have zero leads. But I have a friend in Napa who put me in contact with a Lieutenant Douglas on the police force there who told me a couple of interesting things—off the record. When they first searched his house, they found his wallet and his passport. So they initially assumed that he was still in the US, and they have been working on a theory that he had been kidnapped. But then they got a search warrant for his Google history and saw that just before he disappeared, he had been searching extensively for overseas flights to Europe and South America."

"Really? They can do that?" Sarah asked. "The police can just look through your internet search history?"

"Oh, worse than that," Ben said. "They were able to get into his Google Incognito search history and saw that he'd been researching how to get a fake passport and how to disappear overseas."

"Wow! I thought Incognito was encrypted."

"Yeah, well," Ben shrugged. "Anyway, the reason that this Lieutenant Douglas told me all this was because of Dr. Gaye's daughter, Lenore Gaye. When I told him that I was trying to get an interview with her, he admitted that he was aware of that. Evidently, she told him that she had received my letter and that she was going to call me. The police have been in close contact with her, because they're still working on the kidnapping theory. But no kidnapper has contacted her. So this Douglas guy and I worked out a deal: he would keep me updated—off the record—if I promised that, in the event it is a kidnapping, that I won't publish any details about the case until the case is resolved. He is just wants to make sure I don't publish anything prematurely."

"Can you do that?"

"Do what?" Ben asked.

"Agree not to publish something? What if you get a breaking story?"

"Well, it's a delicate agreement. But I wouldn't want to risk someone's life over a breaking story. Besides, my editor is more interested in the bigger, in-depth story, maybe something we could pitch to Frontline or 60 Minutes in a few months. That is, if the story develops. All I have so far is a promising new drug and a missing developer. I'm just hoping Lenore Gaye calls me."

CHAPTER FIVE

Villa Rosario, Panama

Dan Landes had managed to squeeze a little more information out of Disraeli Gaye, such as his date of birth and address back in the States. Dan and don Fernando then left the prisoner in the holding cell and went back to don Fernando's office. Dan sat down at don Fernando's computer and started searching the internet. After a few minutes, he looked up from the computer screen.

"Well, he's telling the truth—his real name *is* Disraeli Gaye. Look at these newspaper articles I found."

Don Fernando walked around the desk behind Dan and looked over his shoulder at an article on the screen that had a photo of Disraeli Gaye, the same man in the holding cell.

"That's him!" don Fernando said.

"He's a scientist," Dan said. "This article is all about some fancy research project he's doing in California. And here's another article that talks about his disappearance from his home. Is this computer hooked up to a printer? I'd like to print this out."

"Just hit *print*, Dani. The printer is in the break room."

"I'll print two copies of each," Dan said as he hit some buttons on the keyboard.

"I'll get them," don Fernando said, and left the room.

Dan stood up from don Fernando's computer, walked around the desk, and took a seat in one of the chairs facing the desk. Don Fernando returned with the articles and handed a copy to Dan. Both men sat quietly and read through the articles carefully.

Don Fernando looked up. "What do you think, Dani?"

"I don't know, don Fernando. He's not your average tourist, that's for sure. It looks like he's fairly well-known in the States. So what's he doing in La Chorrera? Nothing really adds up. He's not in his right mind, but *he knows* he's not telling us everything... Of course, even rich and famous people can go crazy... except, someone *did* take a shot at him... And he's clearly afraid of someone. He's got a counterfeit passport, and it's a pretty good counterfeit. Well-known scientists usually don't mix with counterfeiters. None of these pieces fit."

Just then, the intercom on don Fernando's desk buzzed.

"Capitán, Dr. Mendoza is here to see you."

"Ah yes, thank you sergeant," don Fernando said, "please send him back."

"Who's this?" Dan asked.

"Dr. Mendoza, from the Solano Hospital in La Chorrera. A personal friend. I asked him to come by and give the prisoner a medical check-up."

Dan nodded. "Oh yes. Good idea."

Dr. Mendoza appeared in the doorway. He was impeccably dressed in a suit, even wearing a tie, despite the hot Panamanian weather. He carried a traditional black doctor's medical bag. Behind him stood an attractive young nurse in uniform.

"José," beamed Dr. Mendoza in a deep booming voice. "Good to see you!"

"Carlos! Come in," don Fernando said and stood up.

Dan also stood as don Fernando made introductions. After a round of hand-shaking, Dr. Mendoza said, "And this pretty young thing is Nurse Sofia."

While Dan nodded hello to the nurse, Dr. Mendoza turned to don Fernando and said with a wink, "She is... *in training.*"

"I see," said don Fernando, and he nodded hello to the nurse.

"Now, where is this patient?" Dr. Mendoza asked loudly.

"He is back in the holding cell, Carlos. We arrested him this morning—for his own safety. He was wandering the streets and talking strangely."

"Well, let's go say hello!" said Dr. Mendoza.

The three men and nurse Sofia left don Fernando's office and walked down the hallway. They had to pass by the desk sergeant and a few officers who were in the front waiting room to get to the holding cell area. All the officers watched Nurse Sofia walk by. Very few women came to the police station, and certainly none as attractive as this nurse in her tight white uniform.

When they got to the holding cell, Disraeli Gaye was lying down. He had reverted to staring at the ceiling and muttering to himself.

When the four people entered the cell, a look of panic came over Dr. Gaye's face. He sat straight up in the bed and said to Dan, "You promised to protect me!"

"It's okay," said Dan. "This man is a doctor. He and his nurse are just here to make sure you are doing okay. Dr. Disraeli Gaye, permit me to introduce Dr. Carlos Mendoza."

Dr. Mendoza smiled broadly, stuck out his hand, and said loudly, "*Doctor* Gaye? Excellent! Always glad to meet another member of the medical profession. I'm doctor Carlos Mendoza, but you can call me Carlos. And this is Nurse Sofia. We're just going to give you a little check-up."

Dr. Mendoza kept his hand extended a full twenty seconds while Dr. Gaye just stared at it. Finally, Dr. Gaye reached out and gave it a small shake.

Dr. Mendoza continued talking in his deep voice. "I'm sure you understand, doctor, that it's just the health regulations of this country, that all *guests* of the police must have a physical. I apologize for the inconvenience and hope you will indulge me."

He pulled a stethoscope out of his medical bag. "Now if you could just unbutton your shirt and let me listen to your heart."

Dr. Gaye glanced at Dan again. Dan nodded that it was okay. Then Dr. Gaye slowly unbuttoned his shirt.

"Excellent," Dr. Mendoza said and placed his stethoscope on Dr. Gayle's chest.

After listening at several places on Dr. Gaye's chest and back, Dr. Mendoza said, "Okay. Now, Nurse Sofia is going to take your blood pressure."

Dr. Gaye sat quietly while the nurse placed a small electronic blood pressure machine on his wrist and activated it.

"One forty-three over eighty-four," Nurse Sofia said, reading the screen on the device.

"Thank you, nurse," said Dr. Mendoza. "One forty-three over eighty-four... not bad for a man of your age, and especially considering the stress of being where you are. Do you know where you are?"

Dr. Gaye looked around at the bars on his jail cell. "Jail," he said slowly.

"Correct. But only temporarily, and only for your protection. Tell me, sir, do you take any medication?"

"Depravity and corruption," said Dr. Gaye flatly and buttoned up his shirt.

"No, no, not *symbolic* medication," Dr. Mendoza responded cheerfully. "Do you take any *actual* medication? Do you take *prescribed* medication?"

Dr. Gaye seemed to think for a moment. A look of sudden realization seemed to come over his face. "Medication... Yes! I need my medicine!"

"Do you have medication with you here in Panama?" asked Dr. Mendoza.

Dr. Gaye nodded his head fast.

"Were you staying at a hotel? Are your prescriptions at your hotel?"

Dr. Gaye nodded again.

"Okay, well, we'll see what we can do," said Dr. Mendoza. "Now, how about any recent accidents? Any head injuries? Any falls?"

"Like Icarus?" Dr. Gaye asked.

"Like, *actual* falling down. Have you fallen down recently?"

Dr. Gaye shook his head.

"Okay," said Dr. Mendoza, taking a more intimate tone. "So… what's been going on with you? How did you end up in this jail cell?"

Dr. Gaye's eyes got wide. "The Synoids are trying to kill me," he blurted. "They've been following me. They are trying to kill me!"

"Someone *did* try to shoot him," Dan interjected.

Dr. Mendoza turned and looked at Dan. "Really?" he said and rubbed his chin. "Interesting." He turned back to Dr. Gaye and asked, "And who exactly are the Synoids?"

Dr. Gaye's eyes grew wide. "I cut into the Synoid and saw their future bleed out. They sent their agents to stop me from cutting. I had to flee. But the Synoid found me. They paid off the trustees and found me. They want to going to kill me and stop my work. I wanted to expose them, but they control the media! They control the government and everything you hear! All my research is going to be sold down the river of Nepenthe. I saw the future, and now the Synoid wants to stop me. The Synoid pumps out Nepenthe to control the useless population. There's no stopping it… I didn't realize… I thought I could stop it, but I had the formula wrong."

Dr. Mendoza held up his hands in a stop gesture. "Whoa, whoa, whoa. That's *way* too much information."

But Dr. Gaye continued. "But I had the formula wrong, don't you see? I thought I could change the pathways for the catecholamines and trace amines. But the tyramines are reverting to phenethylamines. I thought it was an imbalance, but it's really just a different type of balance."

"Tyramines and phenethylamines, eh?" said Dr. Mendoza. "What are you trying to do—make dopamine?"

"Yes!" shouted Dr. Gaye. "But not *make* it. *Replace* it. I had the holy grail of Icarus in my hands, but I lost it. I have to go back into the past and reverse the formula before the Synoid finds out."

"I see," said Dr. Mendoza slowly. "Well, tell me—doctor to doctor—what can we do to make your situation better?"

"Keep the Synoids away!"

"Yes, well, I think we've accomplished that. You're safe here. This isn't the Hilton, but I can guarantee you that you are safe here. We'll try to make you comfortable. Do you want us to call the embassy for you?"

"No, no!" Dr. Gaye shouted. "They're full of Synoids!"

"Okay, okay," said Dr. Mendoza in a soothing voice. "That's not a problem. We won't call them. Let me ask you this, doctor. What if I give you some medicine, something to calm you down? Just to take the edge off? Would you take some medicine if I prescribe it?"

"Yes, medicine. I need my medicine," Dr. Gaye said and nodded and stared at the floor.

"Okay, well, one last thing, doctor. We're going to have to take a blood sample, you understand? Before we can give you your medicine, we have to see what's already in your blood. Can we do that? Will you let us do that?"

Dr. Gaye looked up and just stared at Dr. Mendoza.

"Nurse Sofia here will take a sample of your blood. She's had a lot of practice, and she's getting really good at it. It won't hurt a bit. She's a very pretty nurse, don't you agree? Would you let her take a blood sample?"

Dr. Gaye looked over at Nurse Sofia.

"Now, just roll up your sleeve," Dr. Mendoza said.

Dr. Gaye rolled up his sleeve.

"Now, just extend your arm and make a fist," Dr. Mendoza said. "Now, Nurse Sofia, do you see this nice vein here? Yes, now go ahead and put the tourniquet on... Good. Yes, that's right—swab the vein first... yes, good. Now, Dr. Gaye, while Nurse Sofia is taking a blood sample, I want to ask you a few more questions. You said you were staying at a hotel? What hotel were you staying at?"

Dr. Gaye winced as Nurse Sofia stuck the needle in his arm. "Las Palmas," he said.

"Ah, yes, the Las Palmas Hotel in La Chorrera, a nice place. Very comfortable... Yes, nurse, now release the tourniquet before withdrawing the needle. Yes, well done, nurse. Yes, put the cotton ball over the vein and close the patient's arm. Now, Dr. Gaye, just hold your arm up like this for a moment. Good. Now Dr. Gaye, how did you get from La Chorrera to Villa Rosario?"

Dr. Gaye frowned. He looked like he was trying to remember, but he said nothing.

"Okay, now Nurse Sofia, you can apply tape over the cotton ball. That's good. Well done, nurse. Okay, well now, Dr. Gaye. I am going to take this blood sample to the laboratory in La Chorrera, but I will be back this afternoon, and we will see about getting you started on your medications. In the meantime, just relax. Even though this is a jail, you're in good hands here.

And with that, Dr. Mendoza stood up, and he and Nurse Sofia, and Dan and don Fernando left the holding cell, leaving Dr. Gaye sitting on the bed, still staring at the floor. The guard locked the cell door behind them with a large clank.

As they walked through front area of the police station, all the officers again stopped what they were doing and fixed their eyes on Nurse Sofia.

"An interesting case, José," Dr. Mendoza said as they walked into don Fernando's office.

"What do you think, Carlos? Is he crazy?" don Fernando asked.

"No. He is very agitated, but not crazy. He is oriented in all four spheres of self, place, time, and situation. He knew he was in jail. He understands status relationships. He recognized that I was a doctor, and he behaved accordingly. He understood my questions. He is only crazy in the sense that something is driving him crazy. My experience with people having these paranoid episodes is that there is often a lot of truth in what they are trying to say, but their brains are overloaded, and they can't explain things logically. They are trying to add meaning to *too many* things, and the only way the brain can do that is to use symbolic language to express things. *He* understands what he is saying, but *we* don't. He talked about the 'river of Nepenthe,' remember? Well, Nepenthe is an ancient drug in Greek myth that takes away sorrow... Do we know what type of medical work he did back in the States?"

Dan spoke up. "According to some articles I found, he was doing research on addiction, trying to find ways to treat drug addiction."

"Ah, yes! You see? And what is drug addiction but a way to wash away the sorrows of the world?" Dr. Mendoza said.

"And the Synoid?" Dan asked.

"Who knows?" Dr. Mendoza responded. "But you say someone took a shot at him? Where did this happen?"

"At his hotel in La Chorrera," don Fernando responded.

"Okay, okay. Well, speaking of his hotel, his prescriptions are probably there, and I would like to know what medicines he has been taking. Could you have one of your officers go to the hotel and gather up all his prescription bottles?"

"We're way ahead of you, Carlos," don Fernando said, and reached down under his desk and pulled up a small cardboard box. "When we picked up this man, we found his hotel key on him. So we knew where he had been staying. We thought he might have taken some illegal drugs, which is why he was so crazy. I had the La Chorrera police search his hotel room. They didn't find any drugs, but they did find these prescriptions."

Dr. Mendoza went over to the box and picked up each bottle.

"Okay, let's see... here's Irbesartan, and here's Lipitor... blood pressure and statin medicines, pretty common for someone his age... and this one is for Atenolol... that's another blood pressure medicine... and this bottle is just vitamins... and this one is..."

Dr. Mendoza held up a large bottle and read the label. "Well, I don't know what this is... It's not from a pharmacy. It's from Stanford University, in the US... and it's labeled Dopa. And it's marked as an experimental drug."

"That's what the article talked about," Dan interjected. "It said this doctor was overseeing research at Stanford University on a drug called Dopa, testing whether it would stop addiction in drug addicts."

"Oh-kay," said Dr. Mendoza slowly. "But why would he have it with him here in Panama? Was he taking it *himself*? And if so, why? Was *he* addicted to drugs?"

"The La Chorrera police didn't find any illegal drugs in his hotel, and they did a thorough search," said don Fernando. He pointed to the bottles in the cardboard box. "But I sent samples from all of these bottles, including this Dopa bottle, to the Toxicology Laboratory in Panama City to be analyzed, just to make sure none of these pills were illegal drugs."

"Good," said Dr. Mendoza. "Well, I am going to take this blood sample to the lab in the Solano Hospital. I'll be back this afternoon with the results. We will know for sure if he has taken some street drug. Then we can try to calm him down, reduce his anxiety so he can communicate more clearly with us."

Dr. Mendoza reached into his medical bag and took out a prescription pad and wrote something on it. Then he tore the page off the prescription pad and held it out to the nurse.

"Nurse Sofia," he said, "darling—there's a pharmacy across the street. Would you take this prescription there and see if they have this medicine in stock. If not, we'll get some in La Chorrera and bring it back this afternoon. But if they do have it here, go ahead and get the prescription filled. It's not expensive."

He pulled a twenty-dollar bill from his wallet. "This should cover it," he said. "Bring me a receipt."

Nurse Sofia flashed a big smile, took the prescription and the money, and sashayed out of the room. All three men watched her leave.

"She's a beauty, Carlos," don Fernando said.

"Ah yes, everyone has their weakness," Dr. Mendoza sighed, "and I cannot resist a beautiful woman in a nurse's uniform."

"What's the prescription?" Dan asked.

"It's for Sulpiride," said Dr. Mendoza. "In large doses, it's an anti-schizophrenia drug, but in smaller doses, it just reduces anxiety. It is a very safe drug, and I'm only giving him a medium dose."

Dr. Mendoza picked up the bottle of Dopa again, shook his head, placed it back in the cardboard box, and said. "We need to make sure he stays on his regular prescriptions for high blood pressure. But let's keep this Dopa medicine away from him until we find out what's in it. You said you had read some articles on the good doctor—do you have them? Can I see them?"

Dan handed him the print-outs of the articles. Dr. Mendoza read through each page slowly, then put the articles down and thought for a moment.

"A very high-profile research project," he said. "Normally, I would say that this patient was overworked, that he suffered what used to be called 'a nervous breakdown' from the stress. But the fact that he was shot at, well, that changes the picture. You know what they say: just because you're paranoid doesn't mean you're not right." Dr. Mendoza paused, then added, "Of course, on the other hand, it could just be a coincidence. Maybe he pissed somebody off, or maybe the bullets were not even intended for him, but it scared him enough to trigger a paranoid episode. It's hard to say. That's why I'm glad I don't have your job, José."

Just then Nurse Sofia appeared in the door with a paper bag. "Here's the prescription," she said and smiled.

"Ah, good job. Thank you, Nurse Sofia," Dr. Mendoza said. He took the prescription out of the bag and handed it to don Fernando. "Hold on to this until I get back. If his blood work is negative, then give him one of these tablets a day, along with his regular blood pressure medicine. But don't give him this Dopa drug until we find out what's in it. I'll be back in about two hours, and we can talk some more."

CHAPTER SIX: INTERLUDE

Reno, Nevada

Darryl woke up feeling worse than he had ever felt in his whole life. He had lost everything at the casinos. He was at the end of his rope. He rolled over in the bed and hoisted himself up to a sitting position. He felt so weak. He knew he should eat something, but there was no food in the kitchen. The rent was due tomorrow, but he had no money to pay it. He had tried calling yesterday to see if he could get his old job back, but the boss had just hung up on him. None of his old friends would talk with him either. Over the last three months, he had borrowed money from every one of them. Now they all avoided him. There was nowhere to turn. He was dead broke.

There was a sick laugh inside his head, mocking him. "*Dead* broke? You might as well be dead," it said.

He thought about all the money he had spent at the craps table. He had actually been a couple of bucks ahead a few months ago. Why hadn't he quit then? All that money... gone. He had pawned everything of value that he had, except for that old pistol.

"Good thing you kept that," the voice in his head said.

* * *

San Francisco, California

The Intake Counselor at the Detox Center stared at Steven and just shook her head slowly back and forth. "You graduated from detox and went out and got high the very same day, Steven," she said. "The *very same* day!" That's the third time this year that you've been through detox with us. We can't take you back for a fourth time, Steven. You know our policy. We've got a waiting list of people trying to get in here. We just don't have a bed for you this time."

Steven looked at his hands. "Where am I supposed to go?" he asked softly.

* * *

Bangkok, Thailand

It was Richard's second week in Bangkok. He sat in his hotel looking at his finances. He had burned through almost all the cash he had brought for his vacation, and he still had a week to go. He would have to find an ATM, maybe take an advance on a credit card. These damn ladyboys were expensive. He felt the inside of his mouth with his tongue. That little sore was still there. Maybe he would go to a pharmacy today and get some kind of antiseptic mouthwash or something. He should take it easy today, he thought. He had had trouble getting an erection last night. He was probably just overdoing it. That's probably it. Besides, that little *katoey* last night didn't really turn him on. Or was that one from the night before—he couldn't remember. Who *had* he fucked last night? Or yes, that skinny one. Yes, that hadn't gone well either. Richard got up, went into the bathroom and looked at his face. He looked haggard. He went back to bed and lay down.

* * *

Charlotte, North Carolina

Madeline's husband had gone through the trash and found the past-due notices from the credit cards. He confronted her that night. Even the neighbors heard him yelling. It got worse the next day when he called the bank and learned that the money they had set aside for retirement was almost gone. She had spent it all on lottery tickets. Now he was demanding a divorce. He had stormed out of the house, saying he was going to get a lawyer.

* * *

Tulsa, Oklahoma

After Martin blew into the breathalyzer, the cop put the handcuffs on him and placed him in back of the patrol car. Martin found it hard to hold his head up. Everything was spinning.

"Was anyone hurt?" Martin asked the officer.

The cop looked at Martin and then pulled a card out of his pocket and read, "You have the right to remain silent. Anything you say can and will be used against you. You have the right to a lawyer. If you cannot afford a lawyer, one will be appointed for you."

* * *

CHAPTER SEVEN

Napa, California

Lenore Gaye had waited almost two weeks before she called Ben Wozniak. She wanted to call earlier. She was familiar with ProPublica and liked their work. But Lieutenant Douglas kept dissuading her, saying that if this was a kidnapping, that having a reporter poking around might spook the kidnappers. After ten days had gone by with no ransom note or contact, Lenore decided to call Ben. She was hoping that maybe he could uncover some lead that the police had missed.

And so it was that Ben caught a flight out to Oakland, California, and then rented a car for the drive up to Napa. He met with Lenore Gaye the next morning.

He wasn't sure what to expect. After all, this was Napa County, land of million-dollar boutique wine vineyards and expensive homes, and Lenora's father was well-known in the scientific community. But Lenore lived in a modest frame house north of Napa near Oakville. She was the divorced mother of two, and she impressed Ben as a down-to-earth person.

As was his practice, Ben brought no recording equipment to his first meeting with Lenore Gaye. Nor did he take any notes. He was solely interested in developing some type of rapport with her, getting background information, and building trust. Lenore brought out a photo album of pictures of her father from her youth, and they showed a happy family. She talked about having a normal childhood, growing up in what had been farm country, before the vineyards and wine conglomerates took over. She said that her parents had doted on her and her brother, and had made sure they received a good education. After her mother passed away a few years ago, her father had thrown himself into his work, and that work had been the development of Dopa.

But that all changed, she told Ben, about three months ago. The clinical trials of Dopa at Stanford University were in full swing, and the preliminary results were looking very promising, even better than expected. But her father's mood began to change. Lenore had assumed it was the stress of the clinic trials. But he always seemed on edge, almost paranoid. He still came by to visit her and the grandkids each week. But whereas he used to text before he left the lab, he started calling ahead of time. She asked him about that once, and his terse reply was that texting wasn't safe.

Ben asked her if she knew much about how Dopa worked. No, she said, she wasn't a scientist. She had no head for math or chemistry. She just knew that her father thought the drug was important, that it could save lives, and she was proud of him for dedicating so much of his time and research to it. She offered to introduce Ben to some of the scientists who worked on the project. She was great friends with all of them, she said. Ben readily agreed to this. Lenore gave Ben some names and emails, and while he waited, she dashed off a text to several of them saying that Ben might contact them. What was a lucky break, Ben thought.

Ben was curious as to what motivated Lenore's father to study addiction. Had he struggled with drugs? Were there any addicts in the family? Did Dr. Gaye have any close friends that were addicts? Lenore answered no to all these questions. She really didn't know why her father was so consumed with the subject of addiction. But she did remember him talking about seeing the fentanyl addicts standing around the streets, bent over like broken statues, every time he drove to San Francisco, and how that much that saddened him. Ben nodded. He had seen some of the same zombies on the streets of Oakland as he had left the airport.

As Ben was wrapping up the first visit, he asked Lenore whether it would be okay to bring a digital recorder the next time, to try and get an actual recorded interview. She hesitated a moment, but then agreed. She told him that she had commitments for the next two days, but that he could come back on the third day, which would be Saturday. That was fine with Ben. He thought he could use the two days to try and contact the researchers in Dr. Gaye's lab.

As he was driving back to his hotel, Ben wondered how it was that Dr. Gaye became so focused on addiction. Lenore simply didn't know. Ben had the impression from her that Dr. Gaye was a man who kept his private world completely private, who played his cards very close to the vest, as the poker players say. Ben had asked Lenore about his hobbies, about his close friends, about his interests outside of the lab, and she drew a blank. She really didn't know her father well, Ben concluded sadly.

Back in his hotel, Ben texted the different scientists at Stanford whose names Lenore had given him. The first two answered politely and professionally, but declined to be interviewed. But the third one, a certain Roger Matton, was more colloquial in his reply and wrote, "Sure, come on down." So Ben made an appointment for the next morning.

* * *

As he drove from Napa down to Stanford University the following day, Ben wondered where all this would lead him. Surely, he wasn't the only reporter who was interested in the Dopa story. Were there other news organizations working on this too? Would some other reporter get it to print first? Was it a good story? Would he be able to write a compelling piece that would interest people? ProPublica had given him a budget, and he didn't want to let them down. By the time he reached Oakland and took Highway 80 across the bay, his anxiety was mounting. He wished he had brought some Xanax with him, but he had left it in the hotel.

The drive down took him almost two hours, because of traffic. Then it took him another twenty minutes to find a parking space. He found the research building, and the guard let him in after calling Roger Matton to confirm that Ben indeed had an appointment. Another guard took him by elevator up to the fourth floor where Roger Matton's office was.

Roger was waiting for him. "Hey," he said as he extended his hand. "Sorry for the extra security. The university has been a little spooked since Dr. Gaye disappeared."

Roger Matton was not what Ben expected. He had driven down to Stanford with the picture in his head that he would be meeting a middle-aged scientist in a white laboratory jacket, maybe with glasses, and a preoccupied air about him. But Roger Matton was young, bearded, and his hair was pulled back in a ponytail. Instead of a white jacket, he was wearing a soccer jersey and shorts. He looked like he belonged in a gymnasium, instead of a laboratory.

"Come on inside," Roger said. "We can talk there."

Roger led Ben back into another room that would have served as an office if it had a desk, but all it had was two plush couches and a Coke machine.

"Have a seat," Roger said. "Want a Coke? They're free."

"Sure," said Ben.

Roger pressed the button twice on the machine and two cans of Coke tumbled to the bottom.

"Here you go," Roger said, handing Ben a Coke.

"Thanks," Ben said and sat down on one of the couches. Roger sat on the other one, facing Ben.

"I'm a bit surprised," Ben said. "I thought all scientists were old and gray."

Roger laughed "Oh, no, it's a young man's game now," he said. "There's been so much advancement in the fields of neurobiology and neurochemistry in the past five years that only the recent graduates are fully up-to-date. All the older scientists are having to go back to school just to keep up. Everyone on my team is in their thirties. Even though Dr.

Gaye was not part of this project—technically, we were doing an independent review of his drug—he still had tremendous influence on the hiring process. He pressured the university to hire the best."

Roger frowned before adding, "I guess that sounds like I'm bragging. I'm not. I was damn lucky to be hired for this project. The competition was intense. Everyone knew this was groundbreaking research."

Ben nodded. He liked this young scientist. He seemed forthcoming and unpretentious. "Groundbreaking, how?" Ben asked.

"Well, the success rate for overcoming addiction is not great. In fact, it's horrible. You know how they say that relapse is a part of treatment? That's because so many people relapse."

Roger paused and asked Ben, "Are you familiar with how dopamine distortion is central to addiction?"

Ben hadn't heard it phrased that way before, but he nodded and said, "I've been reading up on dopamine and addiction."

"Okay, well, the current treatment model for addiction uses four techniques. First, it tries to separate the patient from the habit, usually with a thirty-day inpatient stay, where they can't leave the premises. Secondly, it treats addiction with some kind of medicine. These medicines are all over the map, but there is usually some type of medicine given to patients. Thirdly, they try to reprogram your brain with therapy, or some variation of the twelve-step model, that tries to reinforce self-discipline. And fourthly, they use group support, because we're social animals. And the human brain has evolved to depend on, and be very susceptible to, peer pressure. Almost all treatment centers use this four-step approach in the hope that time, medication, education and peer support will break the addiction habit. This treatment model has been around since 1935, and the only thing that has changed is what medicine is used. And that's because in 1957, dopamine was discovered. And ever since then, we've been developing drugs that target the part of the brain that creates dopamine. The belief has been that addiction changes the way that the brain uses dopamine, and that if we can control that, we can control addiction. So we give the patient a drug that either blocks the release of dopamine like naltrexone, or controls dopamine release like methadone or buprenorphine.

"The problem, as I said, is that the success rate for this treatment model is abysmal. As long as the patient is immersed in the treatment system, they stay sober. But change one variable, and they fall off the wagon. Take them out of their peer support network, or give them some stress, or even just expose them to whatever stimuli they associate with their addiction, and bam! they're back to using. What Dr. Gaye believed is that addiction changes the brain *permanently*—that once the dopamine delivery system has been altered, it can never be corrected—and that the only way to stop the habitual behavior of addiction is to change a different part of the brain that controls not the dopamine, but the repetitive behavior. That's the beauty of Dopa. It doesn't chemically interact with dopamine at all. But it disconnects the brain's dependence on dopamine as a reward system. If you're not a slave to a reward system, you basically regain your free will."

"Free will?" Ben said. "There's a non-medical term."

"But isn't that the opposite of addiction?" asked Roger. "When a person is addicted, they have no free will—by definition. They are a slave to their addiction. But give a person their free will back... and the addiction is no longer a compulsion, no longer an overwhelming need. It's just something they can choose to do or not to do."

"So, it allows the person to ignore their addiction?" Ben asked.

Roger thought about this this a moment, but then said, "No, I wouldn't phrase it *exactly* that way. It would be more accurate to say that with Dopa, the addiction is gone, because the compulsion to repeat the behavior is gone. But that said, a person could take Dopa and then, for whatever reason, *decide* to take their drug of choice again, and they would still get high, but they would have to actually *decide* to use the drug—their rational brain would *have to be* engaged in the decision, because they would simply not feel any compulsion to use the drug. In other words, once you eliminate the compulsion to repeat an addictive behavior, there is simply no motivation to do it... unless you rationally decide to do it. And when you engage the rational brain and think about it, there's no reason to use the addictive drug again because you know how unhealthy it is for you. In essence, the patient on Dopa talks themselves out of using their drug of choice."

"That such a weird way to think about it," commented Ben.

"I know! Our patients on Dopa consistently comment on how odd it feels to be able to think rationally again. Some of our hardcore addicts have to get reacquainted with their brains. We put them through a series of classes on how to use logic, how to analyze a problem, et cetera, because some of them haven't done that in decades. But now they can use logic to deal with the world because Dopa eliminates all the compulsive rituals that they used to depend on to navigate through the day."

"Does it work with all addicts?"

"Depends what you mean," answered Roger. "It works on all types of addictions, on any type of addictive behavior no matter what drug or activity the patient is addicted to. Dr. Gaye even did an experiment with a small group of very religious evangelical Christians... and they stopped going to church! They all reported that they couldn't find a rational reason to continue believing in the version of Christianity that they had once found so compelling. That was a very small experiment, not big enough to be statistically significant, but Dr. Gaye was hoping to set up a large-scale study. He was hoping it would be a useful treatment for those people involved in cults.

"But there is one group that Dopa does *not* work for," continued Roger. "But ironically, that group also confirms how Dopa works. Opioid addicts who have severe permanent disabilities, or who are dying of cancer, or who are in constant pain, or who are victims of horrible accidents from which they will never recover... when given Dopa, those people often decide that being addicted to opioids is better than continuing with their admittedly wretched lives. But you see, that, in itself, is a rational decision. They are in such pain, with no hope of recovery, that being in a drug-induced haze is simply a better option, a more rational choice."

"Wow, that's interesting," said Ben. "Can you explain to a non-scientific person like me, exactly how Dopa works, I mean, what it does in the brain to stop the addiction behavior."

"Well, I could, but I can't," laughed Roger. "When Dr. Gaye hired us, we all had to sign non-disclosure agreements to never explain the neurological chemistry of Dopa. Dr. Gaye was very concerned about the formula for Dopa being stolen and copied. That's why the other scientists on this project didn't want to talk with you—they didn't want to violate that contract. But I went back and reread the agreement and it just prohibits me from talking chemistry, not philosophy. So I can tell you that Dopa blocks repetitive compulsive addictive behaviors, but I'm not allowed to tell you *how* it does that."

"I understand. Well, let me ask you this: what about long-term effects of Dopa, side effects and the like?"

"That's a good question, and the answer is that Dopa is still too new of a drug for us to know what the permanent effects are. The original plan was to study Dopa long-term, to follow our current subjects for at least five years, maybe for the rest of their lives."

"Oh?" Ben said. "Do you mean that addicts would have to take Dopa for the rest of their lives in order not to return to their addiction?"

"Another good question," said Roger. "The short answer is that we don't know yet. We don't understand everything about addiction. And one of the things we don't understand is the effect of *aging* on addictions. Statistically, most people seem to grow out of their addiction as they age... or they *would*, if the addiction didn't kill them first. But if you study people who are addicted to some drug and who do *not* get treatment, and if you look at just the survivors of that group, you see that addiction fades. Statistically, most cocaine addicts stop using after five years; most alcoholics stop after fifteen years; even most prescription opioid addicts stop after five years unless they're in chronic pain. We think this phenomenon has something to do with how the brain slows down the release of dopamine as we get older, but we're not sure. We don't have a lot of subjects to study, of course, because usually the drug or alcohol kills the person before they have the chance to grow out of it. So... would an addict have to take Dopa for the rest of their life? Maybe. But possibly not. We just don't know yet."

"And side effects?" Ben asked.

"None observed so far. No liver toxicity, no heart abnormalities, no symptoms like nausea or headache. Our patients report no problems. There is that change in thinking that I mentioned. Patients report that they feel more rational in their thinking. Mood swings seem to go away. Impulsivity definitely disappears."

Roger paused and smiled. "One amusing side effect," he said, "is that patients report that they find it easier to save money. There's no more impulsive buying, no more wild spending, you see, because that's not a rational behavior. That's why I say that Dopa gives them back their free will."

"What's the longest that your patients have been on Dopa?" Ben asked.

"This study here at Stanford has been ongoing for eight months," Roger answered. "Before that, about a year ago, there was a smaller study at UCLA for three months. But that study ended, and those patients no longer receive Dopa. So, for the longest user, you'd have to ask Dr. Gaye."

"Because he ran other clinical studies?" Ben asked.

"No, because he used Dopa on himself." Roger said. "He's the longest Dopa-using subject. He's been on it for at least four years, maybe five, or at least he was before he disappeared."

"Really? He tested it on himself? Isn't that unethical?" Ben asked.

"No," Roger said shaking his head. "Actually, it's quite common. Jonas Salk tried the polio vaccine on himself first. In some ways, it's more ethical to try a brand-new drug on yourself first, to make sure there's no serious side effects, before testing it on other people. Anyway, Dr. Gaye wanted to experience the effects of Dopa first-hand, so he used it on himself."

"With no side effects?" Ben asked.

"He said he thought it improved his thinking. That's the only thing he ever told me."

"Interesting," Ben said. "What about his disappearance? I talked with the police. They originally thought it might be a kidnapping, but there's been no ransom note. Now they're not sure what happened."

A dark look came over Roger's face. "I don't think he left voluntarily," he said. "Over the past few months, Dr. Gaye became increasingly convinced he was being followed. There were several attempted break-ins at the lab, but our security system thwarted them. There are a lot of people very interested in Dopa. Well, *interested* is the wrong word. Let's just say that there are a lot of people who have a vested interested in Dopa *not* coming to market."

"Really? Why?"

"Well, think about it. The illicit drug industry is the largest business in the world. If you ran the biggest business in the world, and some new technology was going to make *all* your customers instantly *disappear*, wouldn't you want to stop that new technology?"

"You think drug cartels were after Dr. Gaye?" Ben asked.

Roger shrugged. "Someone was after him. We saw plenty of suspicious cars around the research building the past few months. Dr. Gaye reported being followed when he left the building. The University even hired a security team to watch his home."

"So you think he has been kidnapped for a ransom?"

Roger slowly shook his head back and forth. "No, not for ransom," he said. "I think he's been kidnapped to *stop* the Dopa project."

CHAPTER EIGHT

Villa Rosario, Panama

Dr. Gaye scribbled in the notebook that the police had given him. He was writing furiously, trying to get on paper the different formulas that were flying through his brain. He needed to take his Dopa again. Why were the police not letting him have it? He couldn't call the US Embassy and complain because the embassy would tell the Synoid where he was. Who could he call? Who could he trust? There was no one. Maybe the newspapers. Yes, maybe the New York Times could expose the Synoid. He scribbled down *New York Times* in this notebook. But wait... what if the Synoid controlled them? He considered this. Maybe it was worth the risk. Someone had to expose the Synoid. But if he exposed the Synoid, he'd have to go into hiding. Money—he needed money to go into hiding.

He heard the guard coming down the hall. There were more than one pair of shoes shuffling against the concrete floor. Several people must be coming. He slipped his notebook under the mattress. He couldn't let them take his notes.

The guard walked up to the cell door, followed by four people. Dr. Gaye recognized the doctor, and the police chief and the American man, and of course, the pretty nurse. He couldn't remember any of their names, though.

The guard opened the cell door and in stepped Dr. Mendoza, Nurse Sofia, don Fernando, and Dan.

"Good morning, Dr. Gaye," Dr. Mendoza sang out in his loud voice. "How are we this morning."

"*We,*" said Dr. Gaye derisively, "are shitty. Why won't you let me have my Dopa?"

"Ah yes, the Dopa drug," said Dr. Mendoza. "Well, the reason we're not giving it to you is that we're not sure that you need it. We're trying to get you healthy, and we are not sure if your experimental drug helps us in that regard. To put it plainly, we don't know what it does."

Dr. Gaye's eyes seemed to twitch. "It's a psychostimulant that elevates extracellular catecholamine levels and enhances neuronal signal processing within the prefrontal cortex," he said in a controlled monotone.

"Yes, of course," said Dr. Mendoza slowly. "But, um, *why* were you taking it?"

"To test the long-term toxicity effects."

"I see... and what *are* the long-term toxicity effects?"

Dr. Gaye's whole head twitched, then he said, "Long-term is a relative phrase, like a rat in a cage. But I need to take it."

"You *need* to take it? Is it addictive?" Dr. Mendoza asked.

"Dopa stops addiction," Dr. Gaye said flatly.

"But you say you *have* to take it. Why?"

"So I can see the Synoid, obviously."

"I see," said Dr. Mendoza. "Well, I promise you, we have no Synoid here. But maybe, once you get better, we can discuss letting you have the Dopa drug again. But for the moment, we're going to stick to the basics. Now, Nurse Sofia is going to take your blood pressure again."

Dr. Gaye held out his arm. The pretty nurse placed the small electronic blood pressure machine around his wrist and pressed a button. Everyone was quiet while the machine whirled and constricted and then released.

"One thirty-two over seventy-five," Nurse Sofia said.

"One thirty-two over seventy-five," Dr. Mendoza repeated. "Thank you, Nurse Sofia. That's good, Dr. Gaye. That's better than yesterday. Now, the police have some questions for you."

Dr. Mendoza looked at don Fernando, but don Fernando gestured for Dan to go ahead. Dan stepped forward and sat down in the chair across from the bed where Dr. Gaye was sitting.

"Dr. Gaye, we're trying to figure out who took a shot at you last week in La Chorrera. Do you remember what happened?"

Dr. Gaye's eyes grew wide. "I saw the Synoid in the street from my balcony. There were two of them. They weren't level-three Synoid members—they were low-level, you know, *lizard-men*. But I knew they worked for the Synoid. I didn't want them to know that I had spotted them, so I jumped back inside my hotel room and closed the door. But then the glass exploded, and I heard pow pow pow! Out in the street. They were trying to shoot me!"

"Did you get a good look at these two men?" Dan asked.

"They were dark lizard-men with horns," Dr. Gaye said excitedly.

"Had you seen them before?"

"In Napa, in the street, watching me. Wherever I went, they were following me. The Synoid had sent them to kill me."

"Okay," said Dan. "Well... *why* does the Synoid want to kill you?"

"Because of Dopa! They think Dopa is going to free the world. Even I thought Dopa was going to free the world, but I was wrong! The tyramines were reverting to phenethylamines. I was so close to fixing the problem when the Synoid found me, and I had to run."

"From the hotel?"

"No, from my home. The Synoid were watching me. They came to my home!"

"Back in California?" Dan asked.

Dr. Gaye nodded.

"And where are the Synoid now?"

"They're everywhere!"

Dan wasn't sure where his questions were going. But he asked, "Well, so tell me this: how can we find the Synoid?"

"That's easy!" Dr. Gaye said with a sneer, "just look in the phone book."

Dan nodded, and then gave don Fernando and Dr. Mendoza a look that indicated he was done with his questions.

Dr. Mendoza then said, "Well, Dr. Gaye, we need to give the medicine a few more days... I know this place is boring, but you are safe here. My understanding is that they are going to hook up a small TV for you in here this afternoon, so you will have something to watch. Most of the channels are in Spanish, but there are a couple in English. Is there anything else we can do to make you comfortable?"

Dr. Gaye thought for a moment. Suddenly he said, "My daughter. I would like to call my daughter. She can bring me some money!"

Dr. Mendoza looked at don Fernando who nodded yes.

"I'm sure we can arrange a phone call," Dr. Mendoza said.

Don Fernando signaled to the guard, who came and opened the cell so that the four visitors could leave. As soon as they were gone, Dr. Gaye retrieved his notebook from beneath the mattress and starting writing again.

Back in don Fernando's office, Dr. Mendoza looked worried. "The Sulpiride is not working," he said. "He's been here almost week, and he's still moving in and out of paranoid ideation. The Sulpiride should have eliminated that by now."

"Are there other medications you could try?" don Fernando asked.

"Yes, but they all have side effects. They would suppress his cognitive abilities across the board. He would be like a zombie. The nice thing about Sulpiride is that it has no side effects."

Dr. Mendoza paused for a moment, then said. "You know what I am thinking about doing, José? I am thinking about letting him take that Dopa medicine again, just on a trial basis. He keeps asking for it, *demanding it*. Maybe he knows something about it that we don't know. I was withholding it because I couldn't see any reason to give it to him... but the opposite is also true: I have no reason *not* to give it to him." Dr. Mendoza paused to think. "But I think I will give the Sulpiride a few more days. How long can you hold him here, José?"

"Well, I can hold him indefinitely while we investigate the fake passport," don Fernando replied. "But I'm really more concerned about the attempt on his life. We can't have people roaming the street shooting at gringos. It's bad for tourism. If I could solve that case and arrest the shooters, I would probably drop the forgery charge and just deport him back to the United States, and let the authorities there deal with it. But for the moment, the counterfeit passport gives me the excuse to hold him here in the jail. I don't think I want to move him until I make some progress on the shooting."

Suddenly, Dan muttered. "Well, *this* is interesting."

Don Fernando and Dr. Mendoza turned and looked. Dan was staring at his cell phone, just shaking his head.

"What is it, Dani?" don Fernando asked.

"When I asked him how we could find these Synoid people, he said 'just look in the phone book,' so I Googled *Synoid*," Dan said. "Listen to this: 'Synoid Capital is an American multinational investment company. Founded in 1997, initially as a fixed income institutional asset manager, Synoid Capital is the world's largest asset manager with over fifteen trillion US dollars under management.'"

Dan looked up from his phone. "Synoid is a fucking hedge fund."

CHAPTER NINE: INTERLUDE

Reno, Nevada

Darryl sat in the metal folding chair holding his paper cup of coffee and staring at it. There were six other men and two women also sitting in their chairs arranged in a circle. Darryl knew it would be his turn next.

The group leader spoke up. "Darryl," he said, "why don't you tell us about how you came to Gamblers Anonymous?"

Darryl took a sip of his coffee and placed the cup on the floor next to the metal chair leg. Then he crossed his arms, looked at the people around him, and said: "I guess my story is a lot like Tom's. I was out of money. I had lost it all at the craps table. My family refused to talk to me anymore. My wife... well, my ex-wife... had left me. I had borrowed from everyone I knew and had stiffed every single one of them. I had stolen money from work, and I got fired. My boss told me the only reason I didn't get arrested was that he couldn't prove it was me. But it was me. He knew it. I knew it..."

Darryl took a deep breath. He didn't want to cry. "The last day before my landlord evicted me, I sat on the bed with a gun... but I couldn't do it. I didn't have the courage to do it."

Despite his best efforts, tears rolled out of Darryl's eyes.

The group leader spoke up. "I think it takes more courage to come here and face your problems than it does to kill yourself. Go on, tell us more."

Darryl wiped his eyes with his sleeve. "I pawned the gun for thirty dollars. I *had to* pawn it... it was too risky to keep it... and then of course..." Darryl gave a self-depreciating laugh, "then of course, I went and put that money straight into a slot machine and lost it... I had nowhere to go. But someone, I don't remember who—an angel I think—had given me the number for the Gamblers Hotline, and I had kept it in my wallet, and finally I called them, and they interviewed me, and sent me here. Thank God for that..."

The group leader nodded. "How long have you been here now?"

"Almost two weeks," Darryl said.

"Tell the group what steps you've taken to acknowledge your disease," the group leader said.

"I've been trying to follow the program. I wrote letters to everyone I knew, confessing that I was addicted, telling them that I was living here, and asking their forgiveness. I've heard back from two people. Tim took me around to all the casinos. I gave them my photograph and filled out the forms to self-exclude me, so now I can never even enter the buildings. It actually felt good to do that. And I finished the inventory of my moral and financial assets, and I brought that with me tonight."

"Good," said the group leader. "We'll all be sharing our inventories after the break."

* * *

San Francisco, California

Steven huddled in his tent on Myrtle Street in the Tenderloin district. It wasn't cold, but he had his hoodie on and was still shivering. Doodle had spotted him ten Pink Ladies to sell. He had already sold four. He heard a voice outside his tent.

"Hey Cupcake, you in there?"

"Yeah," Steven answered back.

"You got any left?"

"Yeah."

"How much?"

* * *

Fort Lauderdale, Florida

Richard sat in the doctor's examination room at the gay clinic in Fort Lauderdale. His three weeks in Bangkok had gone by in a blur. The doctor walked in holding a piece of paper.

"Well, the good news, Richard, is that you don't have HIV. What you do have is a case of oral gonorrhea, which, to be honest, is not surprising, considering where you've been this past month. Unfortunately, gonorrhea has evolved to be quite resistant to antibiotics over the past ten years. So I'm going to prescribe a very strong antibiotic called cephalosporin. You will have to take it twice a day for ten days, then we'll do another blood test to see if we need to continue with the antibiotic."

Richard breathed a sigh of relief and nodded his head.

The doctor continued. "Now, because this is an STD, we have to comply with the Health Department rules and make a list of all your known sexual contacts since you first noticed symptoms."

Richard frowned. Since he'd gotten back to the States, all of his sexual encounters had been with anonymous partners at the local bathhouses.

"Furthermore," the doctor continued, "you can't have sex with anyone until we get rid of this disease."

Fuck, Richard thought to himself. He wasn't sure he could stop himself from going to the bathhouse. It was simply part of his daily routine.

* * *

Charlotte, North Carolina

After Madeline's divorce, her lawyer helped her through the bankruptcy proceedings. She had to move in with her sister. All Madeline had left was her Social Security money, and that was just enough to cover her basics and pay back her sister for loaning her the money to hire the lawyer. She couldn't play the online lottery games anymore because she no longer had any credit cards. Madeline's sister even made her give her ATM card back to the bank. Now, when she needed cash, she had to go into the bank and stand in line to withdraw money. And even then, her sister watched her like a hawk.

Her life was completely boring. She felt flat and depressed all the time. Finally her sister gave in to her constant complaining and allowed Madeline to buy *one* lottery ticket per day at the 7-11. It was the only time each day that she felt alive, that she felt a glimmer of her old self.

* * *

Tulsa, Oklahoma

The court had sentenced Martin to one year in jail for DUI and Fleeing the Scene of an Injury Accident. Martin's Public Defender told him that if that other driver had died, the minimum sentence would have been at least ten years.

Martin was a model prisoner. His probation officer told him that most DUI inmates were good prisoners simply because they couldn't drink in prison. He was paroled after five months, but he still had to do a year of Post-Release Supervision and attend AA groups. Of course, his wife divorced him while he was in prison, but he had expected that. He found work again and started paying child support. He seemed on the track to recovery. He even got his driver's license reinstated.

* * *

CHAPTER TEN

Oakville, California

Ben was not expecting to meet with Lenore again until Saturday, so he was very surprised when she called him early Friday morning.

There was a sense of urgency in her voice. "Can you come over to talk this morning?" she asked.

"Um, certainly, no problem. But I thought you had commitments."

"I did, but I cancelled them. I heard from father! He called me."

"What?! When?" Ben asked.

"Yesterday afternoon. I've been thinking about it all night long. I'm not sure what to do. It's very confusing. He made me promise not to call the police, but I need to talk to *someone*. Can you come over? But don't tell anyone until we talk."

"Of course," Ben said. "I'll leave right now."

Ben hung up the phone and tried to think. He realized that his heart was racing. He had always wanted to be in the middle of a developing story, to be *in* the action. Now, he wasn't so sure. Dr. Gaye had resurfaced. But how, why, and where? And why had Lenore called *Ben*? Why did she not want him to tell anyone? He looked over at the coffee table with his fancy recording equipment, but decided not to take it with him. His original plan was to record an interview with Lenore, to make some video he could use as background to the larger story of Dopa. But his intuition told him that now was not the time. She had sounded almost panicky. And for some reason she had called *him* with this news. It would be better to find out what was going on and then schedule the video interview for another day. He stood up, grabbed his writing notebook, made sure he had his wallet and some pens. As a last-minute thought, he took a Xanax—just in case. Then he headed out the door to drive up to Lenore's house in Oakville.

Lenore was standing on her front porch when he pulled into her driveway.

"Come on in," she said. "I made some Chamomile tea to try and calm myself down. Would you like some?"

"Yes, please," he said, even though he wasn't particularly fond of Chamomile tea.

He took a seat on the couch while she brought a cup of tea from the kitchen. Lenore started speaking without Ben even asking her what had happened.

"I got the phone call yesterday afternoon. It was so strange! My dad's in *Panama!* First, he talked to me for a while, and then a policeman got on the phone and talked to me, and then I talked to my dad some more. He's *in jail* down there! But the policeman said it was only for his own safety. Oh, and a doctor was there too! I spoke with him for a few minutes."

Ben took out his writing notebook and started scribbling fast, hoping that Lenore wouldn't object to his writing. She didn't seem to notice it.

"Okay, okay," he said. "Let's just take a deep breath and start at the beginning. What time did you get the phone call?"

"About four o'clock yesterday afternoon. I didn't recognize the number—it was obviously from another country, but Lieutenant Douglas had told me I should answer every phone call, because, you know, in case it was a kidnapping. So I answered it, and it was my dad! He told me he was in Panama, that he had to leave Napa because some group was after him. He said a name, but it didn't make sense. But then he said he got arrested, and I got scared, you know. I mean, to get arrested in a foreign country... I've heard stories. But then, a policeman got on the line and told me not to worry, that they had only arrested him because they were worried about his safety because he was wandering the street. And *then*, some doctor got on the phone and said that my dad was suffering from some type of post-traumatic stress disorder. And then, they put my dad back on the phone, and he said he needed money..."

Despite the Xanax and the Chamomile tea, Ben's anxiety was spiking. "Wait a minute: he asked you to send him some money? How do you know this wasn't a scam? Someone using AI to imitate your father's voice or something?"

"No, no, I recognized his voice," Lenore said. "Besides, he was very insistent that I *not* wire him money. He kept saying that this group—Cyanide or some name like that—would know if I wired him money. He said he needed cash and that I should bring it to him personally. The policeman got back on the phone and said that I didn't need to do that, that they didn't need any payment, but then my dad got back on the line and *insisted* that he needed cash. Then I said something about asking Lieutenant Douglas, and he got upset and said under no circumstances should I talk to the police because this Cyanide group had infiltrated the police, and then the doctor got back on the line and said that part of the symptoms of this post-traumatic stress disorder was that the patient could experience some paranoia. But I could hear my dad shouting in the background that he wasn't paranoid. So they put him back on the line, and he and I talked for a long while, and he calmed down, but still wanted me to bring him cash. Finally, another man got on the line. He was an American, and he gave me the phone number of the police station, and said I could call back anytime and they would keep me updated."

Lenore handed Ben a piece of paper with a phone number and several names. Ben copied the number and the names on his legal pad.

"Who are these names?" he asked.

"The first one, José something, is the police chief. I talked with him. Then there is that doctor..."

"Mendoza?"

"Yes, and the last name is the American who gave me the number. He said he was just a friend of the police."

"I don't know, Lenore. There's a lot of red flags here. This whole thing could be a scam. It could be kidnappers who have drugged your father and made him go along with this story. I mean, the story is just so crazy."

"I know! That's why I want to ask you if *you* would go down to Panama."

"Me?! What?"

"I can't go and leave my kids here. I wouldn't know what to do or who to trust down there. But you could go for me. I went to the bank this morning and withdrew five thousand dollars in cash. I want you to go and bring my father back."

Ben stared at Lenore with his mouth open. He was on the verge of panicking. He fumbled with his writing notebook and said the only thing he could think of, which was, "You don't have any Xanax, do you?"

"I do," said Lenore and stood up and left the room.

While she was out of the room, Ben took a deep breath. What the fuck was he getting into? He couldn't refuse her request. This could be the story of a lifetime. Also, the whole thing could be a huge scam. This could be some cartel that has kidnapped Dr. Gaye and is trying to extract money from Lenore, or even kidnap her. If he went to Panama, they could just kill him. He had never been to Panama. It could be completely lawless, completely controlled by drug cartels. Who would protect him?

Lenore came back into the room with a small white pill in one hand and an envelope in the other. She handed the pill to Ben and said, "That's .5 milligrams."

Ben washed it down with his Chamomile tea.

"Thanks," he said. "This is all pretty crazy, Lenore."

"I know. I'm just so worried about my dad." She held out an envelope to Ben. "This is five thousand dollars. Will you help me? I checked the airlines. There's a flight to Panama this afternoon."

Ben looked at the envelope, then at Lenore, then closed his eyes and took a deep breath and let it out. Then he opened his eyes, took the envelope from her and nodded. "Look, we can't... I can't just go down to Panama without informing the police here... I mean, they're conducting an investigation, right? If we... if I go traipsing down to Panama with money to rescue your dad, how is that not interfering with their investigation?"

"I promised my dad," said Lenore.

"I understand. But, in the first place, let's suppose the situation is really what it appears to be: that your dad went a bit off his rocker and is being paranoid—like that doctor said—and the police in Panama picked him up and are holding him for his own safety. Then the promise you made to him is a promise to a person who is mentally ill, and that's not a binding promise! Second, what if it's a scam? What if some group is holding your dad hostage and pretending to be the police, and then I go down there, and they kidnap me? We need to let local police know about this before I go. Third, it may be illegal *not* to tell the police. We don't want to get arrested ourselves. Your dad's reason for not telling the police—that they've somehow been *infiltrated*—is kind of crazy, don't you think?"

Lenore nodded slowly. "I just want to help my dad," she said. "He said he needed money quickly."

"I understand. But that's what scammers always do: they create a sense of urgency. We need to let the police know."

Lenore nodded again. "If you go, I promise I'll call Lieutenant Douglas as soon as you're on the plane," she said. "I don't want him to stop you from taking money to my dad, but I will tell him everything if you go."

Ben thought for a moment. "Okay, that's fair," he said. "What time is the flight?"

"It doesn't leave until four p.m., but you know, you have to get there early and all. It's on Copa Airlines, and it's a nonstop."

Ben looked at his watch. That would give him enough time to go back to his hotel, pack, and most importantly, try to call these supposed police down in Panama himself.

CHAPTER ELEVEN

Panama City, Panama

One of ProPublica's rules for its investigative reporters is that they have to carry their passports with them when they go on assignment—just for this kind of emergency. So Ben was able to drive from his hotel in Napa straight to the airport in San Francisco and hop on a flight out of the US to Panama without a problem. And because Copa Airlines bragged that its flight time from California to Panama City was only seven and a half hours, Ben assumed he would be able to interview Dr. Gaye the next day. However, it took him three days to finally arrive at the police station in Villa Rosario.

He hadn't counted on a two-hour delay in leaving San Francisco; he hadn't counted on the time difference between California and Panama; and he certainly hadn't counted on the jetlag from the overnight flight. When he arrived in Panama City around three a.m. Saturday morning, he felt like shit.

He texted both Lenora and Sarah that he had arrived safely. But then he found the nearest hotel to the airport, and immediately went to bed and slept straight through until early Sunday morning. Of course, it being Panama, nothing ever happens on Sunday, so he had to wait until Monday to rent a car and drive to Villa Rosario.

But all his waiting around on Sunday gave him time to investigate everything that Lenore had told him. Yes, the number that Dan had given Lenore was the number for the police station in Villa Rosario. Yes, José Fernando was the police chief there. Yes, they had Dr. Gaye in custody, on a psychiatric watch. No, the police did not want any money, but they were aware that Dr. Gaye had asked Lenore for money. No, the police did not know when he would be released. And no, he could not visit the prisoner unless Police Chief José Fernando approved it, and unfortunately, the police chief did not work on Sunday. Ben was given an appointment for 11:00 a.m. Monday morning. Ben would have preferred an earlier appointment Monday, but was told no, that it would be better to wait until the police chief had had his morning coffee.

* * *

Ben Wozniak wasn't the only North American who flew into Panama that weekend. That same Sunday, the day after Ben arrived, another airline brought a certain Ron Glass to the Tocumen International Airport in Panama City, Panama.

Ron Glass was not the type of person that you would call memorable. He was short, fat, bald, and wore thick, black-framed glasses, all of which gave him the appearance of being an accountant—which, in fact, was what he was. But he was no ordinary accountant. His official job title was Equity Research Associate for New Acquisitions. His employer was Synoid Capital.

Ron Glass did not like traveling. He did not like going to new places. He was much more comfortable in his office in New York City, sitting in front of his computer and crunching numbers. But he had been tasked to go to Panama and ascertain whether a certain Dr. Disraeli Gaye was indeed locked up in a small-town jail. Ron Glass was well aware of *why* he had been selected for this job, and it was not because his position on the Dopa Acquisition Team was that important. In fact, it was just the opposite. He had been chosen for this job because he was the lowest man on the totem pole. Some boss up the food chain had determined that someone needed to fly to Panama, and that job had been delegated down the line, until it arrived at Ron Glass's desk, and Ron simply didn't have anyone beneath him to delegate the job to. He had received an email that Saturday afternoon from his boss informing him that he needed to fly to Panama City ASAP. A file was attached to the email, and that file contained several documents, one of which was a memo that explained that Synoid Capital had developed a source who worked inside the Napa Police Department, and that source had shared that a certain Lieutenant Douglas had received a phone call from a certain Lenore Gaye saying that her father was being held in a jail in a certain town called Villa Rosario, outside of Panama City, Panama.

    Ron Glass certainly knew who Dr. Gaye was. He had been a part of the Dopa Acquisition Team for almost a year, so he was well aware of how much time and money that Synoid Capital had invested into courting Dr. Gaye. In fact, Ron Glass had been part of the statistical group that had prepared the projections of how profitable this new Dopa medication was going to be. He knew how much Synoid Capital had already invested in making sure the FDA was going to approve Dopa; he had helped determine what price the drug should be set at once it received FDA approval; he knew how many lobbyists were already in Congress lining up support for a variety of government contracts to buy Dopa for distribution to the States; he had worked on the projections for the demand for this new treatment for addiction; he knew that Dopa was going to replace Ozempic as the next new miracle drug; he knew how far the profit margin of this drug could be pushed; and he knew how committed Synoid Capital was to investing in (and acquiring control over) Dopa; and thus, Ron Glass was keenly aware of how important Dr. Disraeli Gaye was. All of which were reasons why Ron Glass did *not* want to be the person assigned to bring Dr. Gaye back to New York and convince him to work with Synoid Capital. If Ron failed at this task, he knew he would never work in the capital investment markets again. Ron Glass did not like pressure, but now he was under the most pressure he had ever experienced in his life.

But he had no choice. He was just a cog in the huge machinery of Synoid Capital, and he had been ordered to go to Panama. His job was to determine whether Dr. Gaye was indeed being held in a jail there, to get him out of jail and out of Panama, and to convince him to accept the terms of an investment contract that Synoid Capital had been negotiating with him for the past six months, up to the point when he had suddenly vanished from his home in California.

He had met Dr. Gaye three times before: once in New York City, and twice in meetings at Stanford University in California. On a personal level, he rather liked Dr. Gaye. He knew that Dr. Gaye could be cantankerous, but there was something mischievous in Dr. Gaye's smile, even when he was being difficult. But that was only on the personal level. On the business level, Dr. Gaye was just another opponent who had to be conquered, cajoled, convinced, sweet-talked, or tricked into signing legal documents that would make Dr. Gaye a rich man but would make Synoid Capital even richer.

And so it was that Ron Glass flew from New York City to Panama City that Sunday morning. He didn't know how long this trip was going to take, so he brought two suitcases, complete with two dark suits, seven white shirts, two pairs of shoes, and a folder full of legal contracts. He needed to succeed. He needed to get Dr. Gaye out of jail, to get whatever charges he was facing dismissed, to get Dr. Gaye on a plane back to the States, and most importantly, to get Dr. Gaye's signature on the actual Contract of Investment.

Unbeknownst to Ron Glass, there was another passenger on that very same airplane heading to Panama City this particular Sunday morning—a certain Carlton Jimenez. Coincidently, Carlton Jimenez was also an employee of Synoid Capital, although not officially on any payroll. In fact, Carlton Jimenez's name did not appear on any Synoid Capital employee list, but nonetheless, he was definitely an employee. Carlton Jimenez was being sent to Panama by the same bosses that had sent Ron Glass, but Carlton's job was different. Every major investment always has a Plan B, and Carlton was Synoid Capital's Plan B. Carlton's job was to follow Ron Glass, to make sure that Ron Glass succeeded in his quest, and to take appropriate action if Ron Glass were to fail.

CHAPTER TWELVE: INTERLUDE

Reno, Nevada

Darryl graduated from the Gamblers Anonymous program, but continued to live in their halfway house while he looked for a job. But he was having no luck. Reno is a small town, and his former boss made sure that everyone knew that Darryl had been fired because he was suspected of stealing to feed his gambling habit. One day, Tim—his sponsor in the program—came to Darryl with a job possibility. The Eldorado Hotel and Casino downtown was looking to hire a shuttle driver, to drive their mini-van back and forth from the casino to the airport, to pick up and drop off hotel guests. It was a boring, monotonous job, and it didn't pay well, but there was the chance to earn tips, and it was a job. Tim's only concern was that the job would put Darryl near, and sometimes inside, the casinos.

"I really need a job," Darryl told Tim.

"I know," said Tim. "It would put a lot of temptation in your way, but I think you're strong enough now. But if they hire you, I want to increase your meetings with us to three times a week."

Darryl nodded in agreement.

*   *   *

San Francisco, California

The ambulance pulled up beside Steven's tent in the Tenderloin District. The emergency service medics found Steven's body inside. He was unresponsive. The medic inserted the tip of the nozzle can of Narcan into Steven's nose and pressed the plunger to deliver a dose of the medicine.
"Bring the stretcher!" the medic called out.

* * *

Fort Lauderdale, Florida

Richard was back in his doctor's office.
"Look, Richard, I'll be blunt with you," the doctor said. "You've got to stop going to the bathhouses until we can cure you. The problem is that the medicine we're giving you for gonorrhea is designed to treat gonorrhea. It's not designed to treat syphilis. In fact, it masks syphilis. If we hadn't done that second blood test, we would have missed the fact that you've picked up a case of syphilis. I'm going to prescribe a second drug for the syphilis. But I'm telling you: no more bathhouses and no more unprotected sex. You've got to use a condom, even with oral sex. Do you understand?"
Richard nodded and looked down.
The doctor handed him a prescription. "Take this for ten days, and continue taking your other antibiotics. Come back to see me in two weeks and we'll do more blood tests."

* * *

Charlotte, North Carolina

Madeline continued to live with her sister. She simply couldn't afford to live anywhere else. She felt bored and depressed all day, every day. Even though her sister allowed her to buy one lottery ticket each day, it wasn't enough. That was only one set of numbers. She was used to buying ten or twenty sets of numbers at a time, usually several times a day. What chance was there of winning with just one set of numbers? Her life felt empty. There was absolutely nothing to do.

She told her sister she was having trouble sleeping, so her sister took her to a doctor. The doctor prescribed some sleeping pills. Madeline told her sister that the pills were helping, but the fact was, Madeline wasn't taking the pills. She was saving them up. After a month, she had thirty pills saved up and hidden in her room. That should be enough, Madeline thought.

* * *

Tulsa, Oklahoma

The day finally came when Martin was released from Probation Supervision and no longer had to attend the AA groups. It felt so good to finally have the whole horrible DUI mess behind him.

He told himself that his one mistake that night was getting into the car after he had been drinking. So, as soon as his Supervision was over, he moved to a neighborhood that had bars within walking distance of his apartment. Now he could walk to the bars and not have to worry about getting a DUI. It felt good to be able to drink again.

* * *

CHAPTER THIRTEEN

Villa Rosario, Panama

On Monday morning, Ben was able to rent a car at his Panama City hotel and make the hour-and-fifteen-minute drive from his hotel to the dusty little town of Villa Rosario. He found the police station and parked across the street by a large park full of tall palm trees. As he stepped out of his car, he felt like he was in some old black-and-white documentary film about Central America. The street was dusty, but the heat and humidity were unbearable. There was a horse-drawn wagon going up the street hauling some type of tin roofing; there was a man pushing a cart selling cold drinks; there was a woman walking around selling homemade jewelry. Ben wondered for the umpteenth time what he had gotten himself into.

He walked through the front door of the police station. Across the waiting room was a desk with a police officer. Ben guessed this was the reception desk and he walked up to it. Earlier that morning, back in his hotel, he had used Google Translate to write out on a 3X5 card the Spanish words for: "My name is Ben Wozniak. I have an appointment with Police Chief José Fernando." Ben handed the card to the officer who looked at it and then picked up the phone and said something in Spanish. Then, without looking at Ben, he said, "Follow me" in English and walked down the hall.

The officer took him to a large room with a table and chairs. There were two men waiting for him.

"Ah, Mr. Wozniak, come in, come in," don Fernando said, standing up and extending his hand. "I am José

Fernando, chief of police. We spoke briefly on the phone last Friday. And this is my friend, Dan Landes."

There were handshakes all around. Then all three men sat down. Ben had already decided that he needed to be transparent about who he was and why he was there.

"Thank you for agreeing to see me. As I explained on the phone, I work for the ProPublica news organization in the United States. I was doing a story about Dopa, which is a new medication for treating drug addiction. It is currently being tested at Stanford University in California. Dr. Disraeli Gaye, who evidently is a, um, *guest* in your jail here, is the developer of that medication. He disappeared about three weeks ago from his home in Napa, California. The police thought he had been kidnapped. But I was in the process of interviewing his daughter when Dr. Gaye called her, and told her that he was here in Villa Rosario. I think that you both spoke with his daughter, Lenore Gaye. Anyway, Dr. Gaye asked her to come down here in person, to bring him some money, but she was unable to leave her children, so she asked me to come in her place. That's really all I know."

Don Fernando nodded his head and said, "We don't know much either, Mr. Wozniak. Two of my officers picked up Dr. Gaye nine days ago, when he was wandering the streets and talking crazy. They thought he was just another tourist who had bought some street drugs and was having a bad reaction to them. That, unfortunately, does happen down here. But the situation got complicated very quickly. We discovered that Dr. Gaye was traveling on a counterfeit passport. When we asked about it, the only thing he would tell us was that some group was following him in the US, and that they wanted to kill him, so he had to 'go underground,' as he put it. The officers who arrested him initially assumed that all his talk about someone trying to kill him was part of a drug-induced paranoia, but we have discarded that theory. First of all, we had a doctor examine him and take a blood sample. It came back negative for any type of illicit drug. Secondly, someone *had taken a shot* at him. Three shots, to be exact. The bullets went through the balcony glass door of his hotel room in the nearby town of La Chorrera. We don't know who was involved, or why that happened. But, when it did happen, Dr. Gaye fled his hotel and came here to Villa Rosario, where we picked him up."

Dan spoke up. "Technically, the police can hold him while they investigate the counterfeit passport, but they are really holding him here for his own protection, until they can get to the bottom of why someone tried to shoot him."

"Wow," said Ben. "That... that's all crazy."

"It is," agreed Dan. "We were rather hoping that you might shed some light on the situation."

Ben pursed his lips. "Most of what I know is about the Dopa project. Dopa is a drug designed to stop addiction. The test trials have been going on at Stanford University for the past eight months, and the initial results have been very promising. Dr. Gaye is a well-respected scientist in the States, and holds several patents on other medicines. But his daughter told me that in the last few months her father had started acting paranoid. One of the other researchers at Stanford told me that Dr. Gaye was convinced he was being followed. And there *were* some attempted break-ins at the lab, and other people did see some suspicious cars around the building. The University even went to the effort of hiring a security guard to watch Dr. Gaye's home."

"*Was* he being followed?" don Fernando asked.

Ben made an I-don't-know gesture with his hands.

"He told the doctor who examined him that he had been taking this Dopa drug himself," Dan said. "Were you aware of that?"

Ben nodded. "I did know that. The researcher I spoke to at the lab told me he's been taking it for four or five years."

"Really?"

"Yes," said Ben. "He was trying it out on himself, I guess to test for side effects."

"And were there any?" Dan asked.

"Not that I know of," said Ben. "He told the other researchers at the laboratory that it made his thinking sharper."

"He wanted to continue to take it," don Fernando said. "But our doctor—Dr. Mendoza—decided that there was no medical reason for Dr. Gaye to be on this drug, so we have not let him have it. He is not happy about that. Dr. Mendoza will be here later, and you can ask him about that."

Dan spoke up again. "Was he having any financial problems, or any type of legal or relationship problem that would cause him to want to run?"

"I don't think so," Ben said. "Lenore—his daughter—told me that he was financially secure. His wife had died, but that was a number of years ago."

"Let me ask you this," Dan said. "Have you ever heard of a group called Synoid Capital?"

Ben nodded his head. "Yes, they're a hedge fund. A privately-owned investment firm. They're pretty big, but they manage to keep a low profile."

"Well," said Dan, "We don't know if it's connected, but Dr. Gaye keeps talking about some group called Synoid, but in a very paranoid way. He claims that Synoid has infiltrated all levels of government in the US. And for some reason, they are after him and his Dopa. He gets worked up whenever he talks about this Synoid group. When he's talking about them, he sounds pretty unbelievable. He keeps insisting that this Synoid group is trying to kill him."

"The Dopa project was at the stage of development where it was being courted by several groups of investors," Ben offered. "I was told that several drug companies had already made offers to Dr. Gaye. If Dopa ever gets approved—you know, by the US government—it's going to be very, very profitable. The researcher I talked to at Stanford said that Dr. Gaye had had several meetings with different hedge funds and investment banks from New York—I'm talking big banks, like Morgan Stanley and J.P. Morgan. They came out to California to see him. It's possible that Synoid Capital was one of the groups courting him. But my understanding is that Dr. Gaye was waiting for the Stanford tests to be completed before he agreed to any financing."

There was a pause in the conversation while Dan and don Fernando considered what Ben had said. Sensing that this might be a good time to change the focus, Ben asked, "Can I see him now? And would it be okay if I give him the money that Lenore gave me?"

"Of course," said don Fernando, "although he can't spend it in his cell. But maybe it will help him feel more secure to have it. He can keep it in his cell or we can put it in the safe—whichever he wants."

The three men got up and walked down the hallway, through the waiting room to the holding cells. A guard opened the cell door for them. Dr. Gaye was lying on his bed staring at the ceiling.

"Dr. Gaye," Dan called out. "We brought you a visitor."

Dr. Gaye sat up and eyed Ben suspiciously.

Ben pulled out a small envelope from his shirt pocket and held it out.

"Dr. Gaye," he said, "I'm a friend of your daughter. She asked me to give you this letter."

Dr. Gaye took the envelope from Ben's hand, opened it, and read the letter it contained. He seemed to be reading it carefully, nodding as he went along. Finally he looked up.

"So you're with ProPublica?" he asked Ben.

"Yes, sir."

"Do you know about the Synoid?"

Ben thought fast. "I don't know much about them, except that they are trying to kill you," he said.

"That's right! Did you bring me money?"

"Yes, I did." Ben reached into the large side pocket of his cargo pants and pulled out another envelope, this one larger and thicker than the first envelope. He handed it to Dr. Gaye.

Dr. Gaye opened it. It was stuffed with cash. Dr. Gaye ran his thumb along the edges of the bills. His eyes seemed to shine.

"Dr. Gaye," don Fernando said. "You can keep this money with you here in your cell if you want, but then, the risk is yours. But if you prefer, we can put the money in our safe and give you a receipt."

"No, no, I'll keep it," Dr. Gaye said, as he continued to strum the edges of the bills. "I may need it here."

Don Fernando looked at Ben and just shrugged.

Dr. Gaye looked up at Ben and said, "They won't let me have my medicine."

"What medicine won't they let you have?"

"My Dopa. Can you talk with them?"

"I don't think I have any influence with them regarding your medical condition," Ben said. "But I can help you tell the world about Dopa... and maybe about the Synoid. May I sit down?"

Dr. Gaye's eyes lit up. "Yes, yes! *You* could tell the world about the Synoid! Yes, please, sit down. Did you bring something to take notes with?

Ben held up his writing notebook.

"Good! Yes, I will tell you all about the Synoid!" Dr. Gaye rubbed his palms together and said, "The Synoid— where to begin? Where to begin? I think I have to begin with tilapia. You know the fish tilapia? Very popular in Asia. They grow them in these giant fishponds in China, Vietnam, and Thailand. It's so popular that it's become a staple in the Asia diet, and it's growing in popularity in the United States. Do you know what else is popular in Asia? Having children. They all do it. But, over the past five years the percentage of male children born is slowly increasing. Every year there are more male Asian babies being born than female. It's a steady increase. Do you know why? Let me tell you. Have you seen tilapia in the stores? In the frozen fish section? It's all imported from Asia, right? Have you ever noticed that all the tilapia are the same size and shape? Every piece of frozen tilapia looks exactly the same. That makes them very easy to package and ship. And do you know how the tilapia companies in Asia get the tilapia to be all the same size and shape? When the baby tilapia fish are born—when they're just larvae, just fingerlings—the fish companies add methyltestosterone to their food. And you know what that does? It causes all the tilapia larvae to develop into male tilapia fish. And why do the fish companies do this? Because male tilapia are bigger than the female tilapia, and they are all the same size. So, when they harvest the adult fish and turn them into frozen fillets, they are all the same size and shape. That makes them easier to ship and more profitable to sell. But, there are unintended consequences. Ha! With the Synoid, there are always unintended consequences. That's how you can spot the Synoid! And what is the unintended consequence of eating these male tilapia fillets? You are ingesting tiny amounts of methyltestosterone. And if pregnant women eat a lot of tilapia—as they do in Asia, because it's the cheapest form of protein—then you start changing the percentage of male babies being born. It's not a noticeable problem now, but just wait another twenty years, and you're going to start to see a shortage of women in Asia. And in another sixty years, a shortage of women in the Americas. And why does the Synoid want a shortage of women? Because the masses are easier to control when there are shortages. The Synoid wants to slowly convert women into a commodity that they can exploit for political purposes. Mark my words, if the Synoid succeeds with their plans, you will see women being sold on the marketplace in your lifetime..."

Dan spoke up, interrupting Dr. Gaye. "I tell you what, Ben. We'll leave you two alone to talk. Dr. Gaye has already shared many of his thoughts about the Synoid with us. When you are ready, just holler at the guard to let you out."

Dan and don Fernando left the holding cell, leaving Ben alone with his notepad and Dr. Gaye. Dr. Gaye's eyes were gleaming. He was just getting started.

CHAPTER FOURTEEN

Stanford University, Stanford, California

At the exact same moment that Ben Wozniak was listening to Dr. Gaye explain the Synoid, Roger Matton was sitting in his office back at the research lab at Stanford University, pouring over a series of recent reports and updates on the Dopa project. Because the drug trials were a double-blind study, he had no idea who was receiving the real Dopa medication and who was receiving a placebo. The participants each had a coded identification number, and only the computer server that was analyzing the data knew who was receiving what medication. According to the computer results, the participants in the study who were receiving the real Dopa drug were doing well. Those participants continued to report a complete cessation of their cravings for their drug of choice, and blood tests confirmed that none of them were using. The group receiving the placebo medication was not doing as well. They were receiving the same counseling and education as other group, but all of them still reported cravings, and most of them were still using drugs. As far as Roger was concerned, these reports confirmed the efficacy of the Dopa medication.

But there was one report that Roger was trying to wrap his head around. As part of the monthly evaluations, participants were given MMPI tests. The Minnesota Multiphasic Personality Inventory, or MMPI, was a standardized psychological test that measured personality and mental health problems. This psychological testing had been added to the project at the last minute, and these test results had not been correlated with any other aspects of the project. All Roger had were the MMPI test results for the entire group. Roger realized he needed to ask the computer programmers at the university to separate which MMPI results belonged to the group that received the real Dopa medication and which MMPI results belonged to the group that received just the placebo.

And the reason that Roger wanted more information was that he was examining the last three months of MMPI test results, and he noticed that there was a small—but progressive—rise in the Scale Six scores over those three months. The MMPI measured psychopathology on ten different scales, and Scale Six measured paranoia. The increase in the test results that Roger was looking at was extremely slight—not even statistically significant—but it affected exactly fifty percent of the participants. And that's what worried Roger.

Roger reached for the phone and dialed the number of one of the other researchers on the project, a certain Alison McPherson. He was not calling her because he was fond of her—which he was—but because she had a better feel for statistics than he did.

He launched into his question as soon as she answered the phone. "Hey, Ali, what's that phenomenon called when statistically insignificant findings become significant when there's enough of them?

"You mean Fudd's First Law of Opposition?"

"Yeah, that's it. Tell me how that works again."

"Well, it's complicated. The basic rule is that, in clinical trials, any mathematical change, no matter how insignificant, becomes statistically significant if the change happens in more than seventy-three percent of participants. But that change has to be consistent over time for at least the latter one-third of the course of the clinical trial, and there's a minimum number of participants—I forget how many. What have you got?"

"I've got exactly fifty percent of the Dopa trial participants showing an increase in Scale Six of the MMPI. My problem is twofold: first, the increase is statistically *insignificant*. And second, the experiment is double-blind. So I don't know if the fifty percent that I'm looking at is a random fifty percent across all the participants, or whether these results come from the fifty percent of the participants who are taking the real Dopa medication."

"And you're worried that this increase is coming from those clients taking Dopa?" Alison asked.

"Well, yeah."

"And these results are over what time period?"

"We administer a MMPI each month," Roger said. "These last three months have shown this increase in Scale Six. It's a miniscule increase, clearly not statistically significant, but...."

"Well," said Alison, interrupting him, "you need to find out which group these results belong to. If these results are coming from the fifty percent of participants who are taking the real Dopa drug... well, then what you've really got is *one hundred percent* of the participants taking Dopa showing an insignificant increase in this Scale for three months of a twelve-month study. Then, under Fudd's Law, you only need one more month of *insignificant* increases to have it become statistically *significant*. What does Scale Six measure?"

"Basically, it measures excessive sensitivity, mistrust, suspiciousness of others, grandiose self-concept, and feelings of persecution," Roger said. "It's designed to identify early symptoms of paranoia."

"Interesting. Well, like I say, you need to find out if this result is confined to just those participants taking the real drug. But then, you've got another challenge, which is to rule out whether there is some other external explanation of why these participants would be feeling this way.

"What do you mean?"

"Well, it's not a question so much of whether the results are significant; it's more a question of what is the meaning of the results. For example, suppose that the experiment has been compromised, and the participants have been able to figure out who is getting the real drug and who is getting a placebo? I mean, you're measuring addiction cravings, right? It would be pretty easy for two participants to talk and figure out who was getting the real drug, because one of them would be free of cravings, while the other one would still be using drugs. Then, suppose some rumor spread through the group that the Dopa medicine they were taking had suddenly been discovered to be toxic. The entire group of those people who thought they were taking the real Dopa drug would have a reason to be alarmed, right? And they would register higher on a suspiciousness scale. Remember the Tuskegee Experiment? Where the public health department secretly injected hundreds of black men with syphilis to see what damage the disease would do? And when the facts finally emerged, it was completely understandable why the black communities were suspicious of public health services for years afterwards. So, if you are getting elevated scores on a test that measures paranoia, you might want to investigate whether there is some other causation for the paranoia before assuming it's the drug they are taking. Or, consider the other possibility: What if the fifty percent of participants who are *not* receiving the real Dopa medication are the ones with the elevated paranoia scores? That might be further evidence that the double-blind aspect of the project had been compromised. Maybe people are starting to get suspicious that they are *not* receiving the one treatment that would cure their addiction."

"I see what you're saying," Roger said. "I'm going to ask the guys at the computer center to go back and correlate all the MMPI test results over the past eleven months with all the control groups."

"Yes. They should have been doing that from the beginning," Alison said. "It's kind of odd that they weren't."

"Yeah, well, MMPI tests are expensive. Dr. Gaye didn't want to spend the money. Even though the university is running the drug trials, Dr. Gaye had a lot of influence over the budget allocation. He didn't want to buy the tests and he didn't want to spend the month to analyze the test results. But the budget committee overrode him, bought the tests, and authorized some basic analysis of the results, saying they would reserve a decision on spending money for more analysis as the project went along."

"That's odd that he'd oppose psychological testing," Alison said. "You'd think he'd want to know."

"He wasn't big on psychology," Roger said. "He always claimed that addiction was a purely physical phenomenon—that on a cellular level, the human brain was just associating increased dopamine production with survival. I remember him arguing that addiction *causes* psychopathology, not the other way around. He used to get into some rather spirited discussions about this in the committee meetings. But anyway, I think I need to dig deeper into these MMPI results. And now I've got enough clinical data to convince the budget committee to approve the extra computer analysis."

CHAPTER FIFTEEN: INTERLUDE

Reno, Nevada

Darryl had been at his job driving the minivan for the Eldorado Casino for six months without relapsing. The casino even gave him a raise. He was even able to walk through the casino without feeling tempted to play the slots or any of the table games. He felt proud of that. But driving the minivan all day was boring as hell. He made the round-trip drive from the hotel to the airport five times a day, picking up passengers, letting passengers out, loading and unloading luggage. The hardest part was always smiling and acting upbeat. He knew that was the only way to get good tips. One of the other drivers introduced Darryl to five milligram Dexedrine spansules. These gave him just the lift he needed to stay cheery all day. They were time-release, so he just had to take one a day. He had gone online and researched it, and five milligrams was such a small dose. It really helped him get through his day. Darryl started feeling hopeful again.

* * *

San Francisco, California

The doctor walked up and stood beside Steven's bed in the hospital.

"We almost lost you, yesterday," he said. "You overdosed on fentanyl."

Steven looked up at the doctor and nodded. But to himself, he only wished that they *had* lost him. He had no reason to go on.

"We've located a detox center in Oakland that is willing to take you," the doctor said. "It's a sixty-day inpatient detox program. Are you interested?"

"I don't have any money," Steven said.

"This is a state-funded program," the doctor responded. "It doesn't cost you anything. But you have to agree to stay the whole sixty days."

"Okay," said Steven. "I can do that." But inside, Steven knew he would never complete sixty days.

* * *

Fort Lauderdale, Florida

Finally, after six months of antibiotic treatment, Richard's blood tests came back negative.

"Congratulations," his doctor said. "It took a while, but you are cured."

Richard smiled. "Thank God," he said.

"These STDs are evolving to be more and more resistant to treatment," his doctor said. "We just don't have enough new antibiotics. That's why it's so important to modify your behavior."

Richard nodded. "I understand," he said.

"Are you still taking PrEP?" his doctor asked.

"Every day," Richard said.

"You understand, Richard, that even with PrEP, you still need to be using condoms."

Richard nodded, but thought to himself, what's the point of taking PrEP if you have to use condoms? The whole point of PrEP is so you don't have to use condoms. But he said out loud, "I understand."

*   *   *

Charlotte, North Carolina

Madeline had lost the will to live. She had squandered all her money on lottery tickets. Her husband had left her. She was forced to live with her strict sister, and that was unbearable. Madeline didn't see any reason to go on. She had been saving up her sleeping pills.

But as fate would have it, her sister beat her to the punch, and died first—suddenly and unexpectantly—from a heart condition. Being her sister's only relative, Madeline inherited the house and her sister's bank account. Suddenly she had money and freedom again. As soon as the probate was closed, Madeline went out and bought a new computer, and started playing the online lottery games again.

*   *   *

Tulsa, Oklahoma

Martin woke up in the hospital, handcuffed to the side railing of the bed. Everything hurt. He didn't know how he had got there. One of the nurses told privately that he been in a car accident… and that he had been driving. Martin couldn't remember any of that. It didn't make any sense. He had rented an apartment near the bars just so he wouldn't have to drive. He didn't remember getting into his car.

*   *   *

CHAPTER SIXTEEN

Villa Rosario, Panama

Ben spent an hour taking notes as fast as he could write as Dr. Gaye talked. Finally, his hand began to cramp, and he told Dr. Gaye he needed to take a break. Ben signaled to the guard, and the guard escorted him back to don Fernando's office. Dan and don Fernando were sitting and talking, and they had been joined by Dr. Mendoza.

"He's fucking nuts!" Ben exclaimed as he walked into the room.

Dan smiled. "When he gets going about the Synoid, he sounds crazy as a loon. By the way, let me introduce you to Dr. Carlos Mendoza."

The two men shook hands while Dan explained, "Dr. Mendoza has been treating Dr. Gaye."

"A most interesting case," Dr. Mendoza said. "We have been trying to reduce his paranoid delusion and his anxiety with medication, but we are not making much progress."

Ben shook his head. "It's sad. He thinks the Synoid is behind *everything*—that they control the internet, that they are listening to our phone conversations, that they control government and education..." Ben flipped through his notebook, looking at his notes. "I mean, he rambled about 5G and 6G, about cameras in our cellphones watching us, about the Synoid directing the CIA and the FBI to profile people, about secret courts with Synoid judges, about how the Synoid wants to erase history, about all elections being rigged, about the Synoid creating bitcoin and online sports betting, and how they're behind the tobacco companies who are putting nicotine in our food... I mean, *everything* is a conspiracy to him, and everything can be traced back to this Synoid group..."

Dan sighed. "Yes, we know... we know."

"Oh, and he really wants you to let him take his Dopa medication again," Ben added. "He says that Dopa is the only way he can see the Synoid."

"Yes, his Dopa..." mused Dr. Mendoza. "This has been such a dilemma. The toxicology lab in Panama City could not identify exactly what was in this Dopa. There were no known illicit ingredients, but they couldn't say what effect taking it would have on a person. I've been torn about letting him have it. There's no medical reason to give it to him, but he seems to want it so badly. And as I said the other day, I don't have a strong reason *not* to give it to him." Dr. Mendoza looked at don Fernando and shrugged. "So... I have decided to take a chance and give it to him, which is why I am here today—to see how he reacts when I give this drug to him."

"Do you think that is safe, Carlos?" don Fernando asked.

Dr. Mendoza just shrugged. "I don't think it can do him any physical harm. As for his mental state, who knows? At least he will stop accusing us of being stooges for this Synoid group by refusing to give the drug to him. Why don't we all pay him a visit, and I will give him one of his precious pills, and we will see what happens."

And so, Don Fernando, Dan Landes, and Ben Wozniak walked back down the hallway to Dr. Gaye's cell, this time accompanied by Dr. Mendoza. Dr. Gaye was sitting on his bed writing in his notebook, but he quickly slid the notebook under his mattress when he heard the shuffling sound of steps approaching.

The guard let the four men into the cell. While the holding cell was rather spacious, it suddenly felt very crowded to Dr. Gaye, with the four men standing there looking down on him. He began to get a little nervous. But then he saw that Dr. Mendoza was holding his bottle of Dopa.

"Well, Dr. Gaye," boomed the voice of Dr. Mendoza, "this is your lucky day. I have decided to give in to your requests and let you take one of your Dopa pills. Get yourself a glass of water."

Dr. Gaye couldn't believe his ears. Was this really true, or was this some trick? He stared at the bottle in Dr. Mendoza's hand. Then he stood up, went to the sink and filled the plastic cup with water. His hands were shaking.

Ben pulled out his notebook, flipped it open to a blank page. While Dr. Mendoza was unscrewing the cap to the Dopa bottle, Ben stepped forward and, in a low voice, asked Dr. Gaye, "What's the Dopa going to do?"

Dr. Gaye did not take his eyes off of Dr. Mendoza's hands, but he replied, "It will let me see the Synoid. You should try it. Then you can see the Synoid, too."

"*How* does it let you see the Synoid?" Ben asked.

"It stimulates the nuclei of the pineal gland to align with my energy signature," Dr. Gaye said, holding out his open palm to Dr. Mendoza.

"And what does *that* do?" Ben asked.

Dr. Mendoza shook one small white pill into Dr. Gaye's open hand.

"It opens the third eye, of course," Dr. Gaye said. "And that is what allows you to see the Synoid." He examined the pill in his hand, then quickly popped it into his mouth, and drank the entire cup of water to wash it down.

Dr. Gaye closed his eyes, leaned his head slightly back, and smiled.

"Ah, yes, thank you, Jesus," he said. He stood there for almost thirty seconds, eyes closed, head tilted back, and smiling. His body seemed to give a little shudder. Then he opened his eyes, looked at the faces of the four men, and said, "If you don't mind, gentlemen, I'm going to sit down." Then he stepped over to the single large chair in the cell and sat down, still smiling.

Dr. Mendoza screwed the cap back on the bottle and asked, "How long before it starts to work?"

"Oh, I can feel it working already," Dr. Gaye said. "It brings a warm calmness as soon as you take it. That's the only obvious sensation—a sort of gentle warmness that envelopes you... like slipping into a warm bath. The other effects are much more subtle." Then he looked directly at Dr. Mendoza. "Thank you doctor... is it Mendoza? Carlos Mendoza? Yes, thank you for bringing me the Dopa. I really needed that."

"And how often do you take this Dopa?" Dr. Mendoza asked.

"Once a day is sufficient, Dr. Gaye said. Then he closed his eyes again, took in a long deep breath, then exhaled and said, "Ah, yes."

He opened his eyes and then scanned the faces of the four men looking down at him. He stopped at Ben's face, smiled and said, "You're the reporter who brought me the money, right? Your name's Ben, right?"

Ben nodded yes.

"Yes," said Dr. Gaye. "Well, thank you, Ben. I'm not sure why I was so desperate to have cash, but I am grateful for your efforts. I think I was harboring some belief that I was going to get out of here and would need to use the money to buy a plane ticket to escape the Synoid. I remember thinking that I should avoid using a credit card because—you know—the Synoid can track credit cards. Of course, I had forgotten they can track plane tickets too, but still... it's good to have cash. Thank you."

"So, you... you still think the Synoid are real?" Ben asked.

"Of course they're real! They tried to shoot me at my hotel."

"Speaking of that," Dan interrupted, "we'd still like to know more about that. Do you feel up to answering some questions?"

"I'm at your disposal," Dr. Gaye said and smiled.

"I asked you before whether you saw the men who took a shot at you, and you said something about them being lizard men," Dan said. "Do you, um, have a better memory now of what they looked like?"

Dr. Gaye frowned. "I don't know what I meant when I said, 'lizard men.' I probably just meant that they looked evil. There were two men, on a motorcycle. I watched them circle the block and then stop just past my balcony... I think I also said that they had horns, but what I meant was that they were wearing helmets, motorcycle helmets. I couldn't really see their faces, just around the eyes. But I had the impression they were Latinos, probably hired assassins. Both were wearing dark jackets. One of them got off the back of the motorcycle and was looking around. I knew immediately that they were working for the Synoid. Then the guy looked up and saw me—I was out on the balcony—anyway, when he looked up, I stepped back inside my room and quickly closed the balcony door. Just as I stepped away from the door, the glass shattered and I heard the gunfire. If he had fired one second sooner, I wouldn't be here... Anyway, at that point, I guess I panicked. I felt I had to run..."

"And why would these two men being shooting at you?" Dan asked.

"That's a long story," Dr. Gaye said. "The Synoid first approached me at Stanford after a press conference that the university had organized right after we started the clinical trials on Dopa. There were three of them, all in expensive suits. Oh, they were so smooth and well-spoken! They represented potential investors, so they said. They represented banks and pension funds, so they said, who were interested in investing in medical research, and specifically into Dopa. But they were really wanting to assess what type of threat that Dopa might be to their business. They suggested a private meeting, but I declined. I explained that I was not ready to think about investments until the clinical trials were over. Then, several months later, Goldman Sachs invited me to a meeting in New York. By then, the clinical trials were well underway and showing very promising results, and I was ready to think about the next steps. I had to be in New

York anyway, for a symposium on addiction, where I had been invited to participate in a panel discussion. And while I was up on the stage, I spotted the same three men in the audience, taking notes on everything I said. Then, when I got to my meeting with Goldman Sachs, *they were in the room!* I discretely asked one of the bankers who they were, and was told that they represented private equity interests that occasionally aligned with Goldman Sachs on select projects. That's when I first began to get a sense of the scope of the Synoid... of the level at which they operate... and how far their reach is."

Dan nodded and tried to maintain his poker face, but he couldn't help but think that despite how much calmer Dr. Gaye seemed to be, he was still harboring paranoid delusions about the Synoid.

Dr. Gaye continued. "Anyway, I had some private meetings with Goldman Sachs, where I specifically told them I did not want those three men involved in any investment plans with Dopa. In retrospect, I was probably too candid. I think the Goldman Sachs bankers ran straight to the Synoid and told them of my position. That probably turned the Synoid against me. The meetings with Goldman Sachs fell apart soon after. We just couldn't come to any agreement about financing Dopa. At the time, I just assumed that I could find other investors—that the world of investment banking had many banks and many players. I did not realize at the time that the Synoid controlled almost all the banks. They had decided that if *they* couldn't own Dopa by investing in it, that *nobody* would have access to Dopa. So, they decided to kill me.

"I see," Dan said slowly. "But if the Synoid controlled all of the banks, why would they need to kill you? If they control all the banks, they could just stop you by refusing to invest."

Dr. Gaye frowned. "That was my fault. Again, I was too candid with Goldman Sachs. When our negotiations were falling apart, I got frustrated, and made the rash statement that if I couldn't find funding for Dopa, I would just release the formula to the world for free... I should never have said that. To the Synoid, that would be the worst-case scenario. If everyone in the world took Dopa, everyone could see the Synoid. They wouldn't be able to hide behind banks, politicians, lawyers, and the millions of their agents, sycophants, influencers, celebrities, and blind parasitic followers... I thought Dopa could cure all that, but of course I was wrong..." Dr. Gaye's voice trailed off. "But anyway, that was my thinking at the time. But, to answer your question about *why* they wanted to kill me... well, the impulse to murder is such a basic human emotion, don't you think? Goes back to Cain and Abel. When someone stands in your way, the first impulse of the human brain in its primitive brainstem, is to bludgeon your opponent, to kill them. The Synoid is no different... The Synoid didn't rise to power because they are more advanced! They rose to power because they are more primitive! They're basically just mobsters—mobsters in expensive suits. I was a threat to their business. So, of course, they wanted to kill me. Despite how messy murder is, it's the most efficient way to solve political problems."

Dan looked over to don Fernando in frustration. Don Fernando nodded and stepped forward. "Dr. Gaye, permit me to be blunt. Villa Rosario is a tiny village. La Chorrera is a small city. We are dependent on tourism. We do not care about politics or banks, or your little Dopa project. We only care about having enough tourists visit us so that we maintain our economy. We can't have people shooting tourists—it is bad for business. So, our *only* interest is arresting the people who shot at you. So please, can you tell us anything else that will help us find these two motorcycle men."

Dr. Gaye furrowed his brow and thought for a moment. Then he asked, "Would their license plate number help?"

"The license plate?" asked don Fernando. "You mean the license plate of the motorcycle?"

"Yes," said Dr. Gaye. "It was MS-2331."

Don Fernando just stared at Dr. Gaye. Then he said, "Are you sure?"

"Oh yes, I have an odd memory, almost photographic, especially when it comes to numbers. It's a facility that has been very useful to me in my career. I noticed the license plate on the motorbike. I assumed the capital M stood for motorcycle and that the capital S stood for Synoid. I don't know what the 2331 stands for."

"Alright," said don Fernando slowly. "We'll check that out."

Dr. Mendoza had been quietly watching Dr. Gaye. Finally, he asked, "Is the Dopa effect always so immediate, always so dramatic?"

An odd look came over Dr. Gaye's face, almost one of sadness. "No, not at first. It's only after years of taking it that the body develops an affinity for it and reacts immediately. Similar to addiction, Dopa alters the brain. I was scheduled to have some MRIs done back at Stanford before I was forced to flee. I was interested in seeing how Dopa had altered my brain after having taken it for five years."

Ben spoke up. "When you say that the body *develops an affinity* for Dopa, what do you mean, exactly?"

Dr. Gaye lowered his head and rubbed his hand across his mouth, then looked up at Ben and said, "All cures have negative consequences, and one of those negative consequences is that a cure always stimulates a disease to mutate. It's pure natural selection. When a disease encounters a cure, it fights to survive by mutating. But in some cases, the cure mutates as well. Dopa is designed to cure addiction. But... it turns out that the cure is addictive."

"You mean?" Ben started to say.

"Yes," said Dr. Gaye. "Over time, Dopa becomes addictive."

There was a moment of silence in the cell as the four men considered what Dr. Gaye had said. Dr. Gaye looked at their serious faces, smiled, and said, "But, we knew that from the beginning, gentlemen. We knew that once someone started taking Dopa to fight drug addiction—that they would have to continue taking it for the rest of their lives. We knew that! We just didn't know that that was also true for people who weren't addicted to drugs. Still... that is a small price to pay for the tremendous benefits of Dopa. Without Dopa, a person can't see the Synoid. Addiction is a small price to pay for freedom, don't you think?"

Ben looked at Dr. Mendoza and then at don Fernando. Ben started to say, "I don't know about that..." when Dr. Gaye interrupted him. "Well, listen Ben, let me explain it this way: Consider the everyday sandwich, like a ham and cheese sandwich, something that we take for granted, right? The bread is just the delivery system for the ham and cheese. We don't give the bread a second thought. But bread was only invented 10,000 years ago, and human beings have been around for 200,000 years. And yet, bread has become an indispensable part of our diet and our culture. We're accustomed to it; we take it for granted. It relieves our hunger. Why shouldn't Dopa be the same way? Why shouldn't Dopa become our daily bread? Dopa can relieve us of the Synoid the same way that bread relieves us of hunger. Think of the benefit to the world if everyone could see the Synoid."

The four men just stared at Dr. Gaye. Finally, Dr. Mendoza asked, "How are you feeling?"

"Fine, just fine," Dr. Gaye responded. "But I think I'm going to lie down now and rest a bit."

Dr. Mendoza looked at don Fernando, who just shrugged.

"Okay," said Dr. Mendoza. "We'll check back on you in about an hour."

Dr. Gaye lay down on his bed, placed his hands behind his head, smiled, and began to whistle a tune. The four men looked at each other. Don Fernando signaled for the guard. As the guard was letting them out of the cell, Dr. Mendoza leaned close to the guard and whispered, "Keep an eye on him. If he seems in any type of physical distress, please notify us immediately."

The guard nodded. Then the four men walked back to don Fernando's office.

CHAPTER SEVENTEEN

Villa Rosario, Panama

The four men—don Fernando, Dr. Mendoza, Ben, and Dan—left Dr. Gaye's jail cell, each feeling frustrated for different reasons. Don Fernando stopped at the front desk and gave the desk sergeant the license plate number that Dr. Gaye had given him. The desk sergeant immediately picked up the phone and began dialing.

When the four men got back to don Fernando's office, Dr. Mendoza said, "I have never seen a medicine act as fast as that Dopa medicine. It affected his ability to reason and converse within minutes."

"It certainly made him more loquacious," said Dan, "but it didn't make him any less paranoid."

"But he was able to remember that license plate number," don Fernando said.

"And our names," Ben added.

"But he's still crazy as a loon," Dan said. "What are you going to do with him, don Fernando?"

"I don't know," don Fernando said. "Our only lead is this license plate number. If that doesn't pan out, then this case is at a dead end, and I'm just going to ask the Ministry of Migration to deport him back to the United States. Let them deal with his counterfeit passport."

Dan nodded. "You know, I've actually gotten a little fond of him. I just wish he'd get off this Synoid kick."

"I know what you mean," don Fernando replied. "He is a likeable person... and a model prisoner. Do you know that he makes his bed every morning? We've never had a prisoner do that."

"Well, don't ship him out right away," Dr. Mendoza said. "Let's give this Dopa drug a few more days. Maybe it needs more time to reduce his paranoid thinking."

"Well, I'll be damned," Ben interjected. He had been scrolling on his phone while the three men were talking. Ben looked up from his phone and said, "You remember that story he told me earlier, before you left me with him, about the tilapia fish? Well, it's true. Well... maybe not the Synoid part... but those fish farms in Asia do give the fish some type of testosterone drug to turn them into males. He was right about *that* part."

Dan shrugged. "All conspiracy theories start with one grain of truth," he said, "before they veer off into la-la land."

Just then, the desk sergeant appeared in the doorway. "Capitán," he said to don Fernando, "I am sorry to disturb you, but there are two matters. First, the license plate belongs to a motorcycle that was reported stolen out of Panama City two months ago. It has not been recovered yet."

"I was afraid of that," don Fernando said. "And the second matter?"

"There is someone here who wishes to speak with you about the prisoner. He gave me his card."

The desk sergeant handed the business card to don Fernando. A look of concern came over don Fernando's face. He handed the card to Dan, who also frowned while reading it.

"What is the matter?" Dr. Mendoza asked.

"It is someone from Synoid Capital," Dan said. The card says he is an Equity Research Associate, whatever that means."

Don Fernando looked at the desk sergeant and said, "Show the gentleman in, Sergeant."

Ben felt torn. He felt that he was overstaying his appointment. He had only come here to talk with Dr. Gaye. He knew that he should excuse himself and let the police talk to this person, whoever he was. But he reminded himself that he was a reporter, and here he was about to witness something. He didn't know what, but he felt that he was going to witness some new—and important—development in the case. So he took a small step backwards and just stood there without saying a word, trying to be as inconspicuous as possible.

The desk sergeant returned, escorting a man dressed in a dark suit carrying a briefcase. The man was short, bald, and overweight. He looked around the room at all four men, trying to figure out who was in charge. The desk sergeant started to leave, but don Fernando made a subtle gesture for him to stay.

"My name is Ron Glass," the man said finally to the group. "I am looking for Police Chief José Fernandez."

"That would be me, señor," don Fernando said. "How can I help you?"

Ron Glass nodded to don Fernando and then glanced at the other three men again. Clearly, none of them were leaving, so evidently Ron would have to make a group presentation. He cleared his throat and said, "Well, I am very sorry to intrude without an appointment. As I mentioned, my name is Ron Glass. I work with an investment firm in the United States, and it is our understanding that a certain business associate of ours is here in your jail."

"And who would that be?" don Fernando asked.

"Well, um, it's Dr. Disraeli Gaye. We were told that Dr. Gaye was being held here."

"And who is we?" don Fernando asked firmly.

Ron Glass was starting to get nervous. "Well, I work for Synoid Capital. Um, we are a private equity group, that is, an investment firm. We were given information from, ah, reliable sources, that our associate Dr. Gaye was here, that he was being kept here on a psychiatric watch."

Dan spoke up. "And how exactly is he a business associate of yours?"

"Well, Dr. Gaye is the inventor and patent holder of a new medicine, that is currently finishing up drug trials in California. And we have a signed letter of intent with Dr. Gaye to have Synoid Capital provide the underwriting, securitization, and marketing of this medicine. We were looking forward to working together on this business venture."

Dan, don Fernando, and Dr. Mendoza all glanced at each other.

"Do you have a copy of that letter?" don Fernando asked.

"Um, well, yes, actually, I think I do," Ron Glass stammered. He opened his briefcase and started rummaging through his file folders. He hadn't been prepared to be cross-examined like this.

The four men waited stoically while Ron Glass thumbed through each of his manila folders until he finally pulled one out, opened it, and removed a two-page document.

"Here it is," Ron Glass announced, and handed it to don Fernando. Don Fernando glanced at it, then handed it to Dan who read through it quickly, turning to the second page where there were several signatures, including one that appeared to be Dr. Gaye's.

Don Fernando looked at the desk sergeant and said, "Sergeant, would you make a copy of this letter for our files?"

"Sí, Capitán."

Dan handed the letter to the desk sergeant who left quickly.

"Mr. Glass," Dan said, "I'm still unclear. Why have you traveled all the way here simply for someone that you *might* be doing business with?"

"Oh, Dr. Gaye is very important to us. We have already invested millions of dollars into preparing for this business relationship. The acquisition of this project is shaping up to be the largest investment that Synoid Capital has ever made. It's a very important medical breakthrough."

"So... you are here to protect your investment?" Dan asked.

"Well, Synoid Capital is here to protect Dr. Gaye. I was hoping to have him released to my custody so that I could take him back to New York with me. We have made arrangements for a psychiatric bed for him at Gracie Square Hospital in New York City. We understand that he is suffering from an acute psychotic episode and, if I may speak frankly, he would probably receive better care in a private psychiatric hospital than here in a jail cell."

Don Fernando and Dr. Mendoza both took umbrage at Ron Glass's assumption of the quality of Dr. Mendoza's medical care. They each stiffened ever so slightly as they tried not to react.

Ron Glass began rummaging through his briefcase again. "I have brought a letter from Gracie Square Hospital confirming that they have a bed waiting for him, and an affidavit from Synoid Capital stating that we will assume all responsibility and expense for transporting him to the hospital and for his treatment there. We just want to help him get better."

Ron Glass pulled out some more documents from his briefcase just as the desk sergeant appeared in the doorway with a copy of the letter of intent.

"I apologize, Sergeant," don Fernando said. "Evidently, we need copies of some more papers."

Ron Glass looked at don Fernando and then dutifully handed the papers to the desk sergeant.

"Señor Glass," don Fernando said, "I can appreciate that you have an interest in Dr. Gaye. However, there are some legal problems to deal with. First of all, he was traveling in our country on a counterfeit passport, which is why he is currently under arrest and residing in a jail cell rather than in one of our many fine hospitals. And I might add that while he has been our guest, he has been receiving excellent medical care on a daily basis from Dr. Mendoza here." Don Fernando gestured to Dr. Mendoza. "Secondly, you are not the first representative from your company who has come here looking for Dr. Gaye. About two and a half weeks ago, some other individuals— reputed by a witness to be from Synoid Capital—attempted to kill Dr. Gaye, using a firearm. And while I understand that that is a common occurrence in your country, it is something we disapprove of here in Panama. What do you know about this attempt on Dr. Gaye's life?"

Dan bit his lip. He was used to don Fernando's inventive questioning technique, but he hoped that Ben and Dr. Mendoza's expressions would not betray how much don Fernando was stretching the truth.

"I-I-well, that is impossible," Ron Glass stuttered. "We just found out that he was here on Saturday."

"And how did you discover that?" don Fernando asked.

"From the Napa Police Department, or rather from a source in that police department. We learned that Dr. Gaye had called his daughter and told her he was here."

Ben made a quick mental note to call Lenore as soon as he could to tell her to stop talking to Lieutenant Douglas.

Dan spoke up. "And how is it that a private equity firm has snitches in a police department?"

Ron Glass did not like being bombarded with all these questions. "Well, ah, naturally, when Dr. Gaye disappeared, we took all the steps we could to find him. We contacted the police; we interviewed our associates at Stanford University; we..."

Dan interrupted him. "You have associates at Stanford University?"

"Well, yes, of course. Synoid Capital is a major donor to Stanford. We were the ones who suggested to Dr. Gaye that the clinical trials be held at Stanford."

The desk sergeant returned with multiple copies of Ron Glass's documents. There was a brief pause in the interrogation while Dan separated the copies and handed the originals back to Ron Glass. Once again, don Fernando discretely signaled to the desk sergeant to not leave.

"Well, señor Glass," don Fernando said, "we very much appreciate your concern for our prisoner here. And we need some time to study these fine documents you have brought to us. May I ask, what hotel are you staying at?"

"The Waldorf Astoria in Panama City," Ron Glass answered.

"Ah yes, of course. That is the finest hotel in all of Panama. I am sure you are comfortable there. We will consider your offer very carefully, but we will need a few days to do so. But we know where to find you, and we will let you know."

Ron Glass realized that don Fernando was wrapping up the visit. He decided to take a different approach. "We at Synoid Capital only want what is best for Dr. Gaye. Our lawyers in New York are in contact with their counterparts in Panama City to prepare legal documents of guardianship for Dr. Gaye. We want to proceed in the proper legal manner, to guarantee that Dr. Gaye can be quickly released to our custody and taken to the States where he can receive the best of medical care."

"Of course, of course," said don Fernando. "That is an excellent idea. I'm sure you will find Panama's legal system easy to navigate and receptive to your efforts. As I say, we need some time to consider the situation. I am sure we all have Dr. Gaye's best interests at heart. I thank you again for coming by and sharing with us. The sergeant will show you out. Thank you again."

The desk sergeant gently took Ron Glass's arm and guided him out of the room.

After Ron Glass was gone, Dr. Mendoza turned to don Fernando, smiled broadly and said, "Ah, José, once again, I am thankful I do not have your job."

CHAPTER EIGHTEEN: INTERLUDE

Reno, Nevada

Darryl continued working his job driving the minivan for the Eldorado Hotel and Casino, but he had increased his Dexedrine use to twice a day. He told himself that it was only five milligrams, and the capsules did allow him to get through the boring job of driving hotel guests back and forth to the airport. They kept him cheerful and smiling for all the guests, which increased his tips. But he found that, at the end of the day, he needed several drinks in order to relax enough to sleep. He didn't like the drinking because that kept him in the casino bar, and he was afraid that he would yield to temptation and start gambling again. So a friend of his suggested he try diazepam. That did the trick! Darryl would just take a two-milligram tablet as soon as he got home from work, and he would start to relax. Life was good.

* * *

San Francisco, California

The ambulance EMT pulled open the flap to Steven's tent, and pulled Steven's body out by the legs. Steven's face was turning blue. The EMT inserted the tip of the Narcan canister into Steven's nose and gave him a dose. After a few seconds, Steven's head twitched.

"He's coming around!" the EMT shouted to the other ambulance worker. The second EMT worker leaned over Steven's body and looked at his face.

"Hey, I recognize this guy," the second EMT said. "We took him to the hospital two weeks ago."

The first EMT shook his head and said, "One of these days, we're going to be too late. C'mon, let's get him on a stretcher."

* * *

Fort Lauderdale, Florida

Someone at the bathhouse had introduced Richard to the practice of using crystal meth to enhance his sexual experience. Although Richard knew that meth was addictive, he figured he could try it once without any problem. But he couldn't believe how much better it made the sex. He could stay at the bathhouse for ten hours having sex with dozens of partners and never get tired. Why hadn't anyone told him about this before? Finally, this was the sexual high he had been searching for.

* * *

Charlotte, North Carolina

Once Madeline had inherited her sister's money, she could play the lottery as much as she wanted. But she soon discovered that buying online lottery tickets wasn't enough. She started going to the Indian casino at the edge of town. She tried Keno, but it was too slow. Roulette intimidated her. But the slot machines were perfect. She could spend hours sitting in front of one. The waitresses brought her drinks and little sandwiches. First she only went on Saturdays, but soon she was going every day. She made new friends. Playing the slots filled her time and gave her something to look forward to.

* * *

Tulsa, Oklahoma

Martin couldn't believe his bad luck. His sentencing judge was the very same judge that Martin had had on his last DUI. His lawyer said there was nothing they could do about that. Martin could only stand there with his head lowered while the judge lambasted him about wasting his last second chance. Three years in prison.
Fuck.
His life was over.

* * *

CHAPTER NINETEEN

Stanford University, Stanford, California

Roger Matton was talking with his associate Alison McPherson again about the Dopa MMPI results.

"I had no problem convincing the budget committee to authorize the funds for the computer center to run the data on those MMPI results," Roger was telling her. "And my fears were correct. These slight increases on Scale Six are all from the participants who are receiving the true Dopa drug."

"That's that paranoia scale you told me about?" Alison asked.

"It's more like ideas of persecution," Roger said. "It measures suspiciousness, feelings of hyper-sensitivity... but yeah, things that lead to paranoia."

"So *all* the patients on Dopa have a statistically *insignificant* increase in feeling paranoid over the last three months?" Alison asked.

"Uh-huh. We're going to have them take the MMPI again next month, to see if this trend continues."

"Well," Alison said, "as I said before, whether the increase in feelings of paranoia is significant or not, you still have to rule out any other cause for that, such as double-blind contamination or a design flaw. But, that said, let me ask you: what will happen to Dopa if you conclude that *it does cause* a statistically significant increase in feelings of paranoia?"

"Well, that's interesting question, on several levels," Roger said. "The basic answer is that it doesn't affect the study. The university will publish the results whatever the results are. However, it could affect the marketing of the drug. The FDA can approve a drug even though it has a psychological risk. For example, a lot of sleeping pills have to carry warnings about suicidal thoughts. But they still are marketed, and they still sell well. The real risk is if the FDA requires further testing—*that* could delay the approval and marketing of the drug for several years. All we've got so far is three months of an insignificant increase in feelings of persecution. That, by itself, would not be enough to even be included in the final report. But if we see one more month of this trend on the MMPI, then, under Fudd's Law, the results would be statistically significant, and we'd *have* to report them. That might—or might not—trigger further FDA scrutiny."

"I see," said Alison.

"On that note," Roger continued, "I had an interesting phone call from one of the university trustees yesterday. A guy named Robert Wesley. I met him once before at some university dinner. He's rich, kind of an ass. Anyway, he's on the board overseeing the Dopa project, but he's not on the budget committee. But somehow he'd heard that I got the budget committee to fund the extra data analysis of the MMPI results, and he wanted to know why. I basically gave him some bullshit about wanting the final university report to be complete. I told him that I was expecting the results to help solidify Dopa's position as a break-through drug. That seemed to satisfy him. Then he kind of slipped up and mentioned that some of the big institutional supporters of the university were looking to invest heavily into Dopa. He actually made some comment about what's good for Dopa is good for the university. I told him I understood and just laughed along with him, but it really pissed me off. I mean, there's supposed to be an ethical wall between these drug trials and any financial interests. I thought about reporting him, but I couldn't figure out who to report him to. Plus, his comments were vague enough that I don't think I could prove anything. But, like I said, it pissed me off."

"How did he find out that you had talked to the budget committee?" Alison asked.

"I don't know. Maybe he's got a friend on the committee, or maybe someone at the computer center ratted me out for making them do extra work. I just don't know. It was the first time someone on the board has ever called me directly. They're supposed to do everything through the board meetings."

"You know," said Alison. "I hate politics. Before I came to work here, I thought all universities were above politics—you know, that they were true ivory towers of science and learning. But since I started this job, I've come to realize that the university research world is just as overrun with political bullshit and hidden agendas as anywhere else."

"I know. It's just that I had really campaigned hard to be on this Dopa project because I truly believe that a drug like Dopa could change the world. I didn't sign up just to line some rich guy's pockets."

Alison nodded her head. "But you know what they say. Money rules."

CHAPTER TWENTY

Villa Rosario, Panama

Don Fernando stared at the email on his computer. It only consisted of one sentence, and it was anonymous—anonymous in the sense that it wasn't signed by a person, but by a gang name. The email read "Release the gringo or we will kill you and everyone around you." And it was simply signed "Sinaloa."

Now, don Fernando had been the police chief of Villa Rosario for more than twenty-five years, and he had not maintained that position by being easily intimidated, or by being stupid. He knew that the Sinaloa cartel did not use emails to extort their victims, nor would they ever simply sign any document as "Sinaloa." The cartel preferred a personal touch, direct communication, spoken threats. He also knew that the Sinaloa cartel did not really have a presence—or an interest—in the tiny and impoverished pueblo of Villa Rosario. So don Fernando knew that this email was a scam, and it was a scam by somebody other than the Sinaloa cartel. But the question was: by whom? And why?

He pressed the button on his intercom and asked the desk sergeant to track down Carlos Wang and send him to his office.

Like many citizens of Panama, Carlos Wang's ancestors were brought over from China to build the Panama Canal. But Carlos was 100% Panamanian, born and raised in Panama. The only difference was that Carlos had a natural talent for computer hacking, and had been recruited and trained by the FBI in Quantico, Virginia, before getting homesick and returning to Panama where don Fernando met him at a job fair. Even though Villa Rosario was a small dusty pueblo, don Fernando understood the growing presence of technology. Most of the town had WiFi, and everyone had a cell phone, even the men who still rode donkeys for transportation. So Don Fernando created a position for Carlos in the police department and hired him.

"Ah, Carlos. Come in," don Fernando said when Carlos appeared in his doorway. "Come and look at this intriguing email I received."

Don Fernando turned his computer screen to the side and Carlos bent over to read the email.

"Very strange, Capitán. I did not think the Sinaloa used email. I thought they preferred to send messages by apps like Telegram or WhatsApp."

"Exactly," said don Fernando. "But my email address is public information and easy to find, whereas my telephone number is very private. So I think this is some other person or other group. I would you to find out who they are, and if possible, where they are located."

"Con permiso, Capitán," Carlos said and moved the computer mouse to hover over the sender's email address so that an email address appeared. "Ah, see, they are using a commercial email masking service. I should be able to find out their true email address. Then I can send them a fake email, and if they respond, I can track down their IP address and a location. Can you forward this email to me?"

"Of course, Carlos. Thank you."

* * *

As the very time that don Fernando was talking with Carlos Wang, Ben Wozniak was listening to Dr. Gaye in his cell and taking notes. Don Fernando had given Ben permission to visit Dr. Gaye each day for as much time as he'd like. Ben assumed it was don Fernando's support of independent journalism that motivated him to give Ben free access to Dr. Gaye. In reality, don Fernando was just trying to keep Dr. Gaye from getting too bored sitting in a jail cell. Dr. Mendoza had supported the idea of a daily visits being good for Dr. Gaye's recovery. And Dr. Gaye certainly seemed to enjoy explaining the inner workings of the Synoid to Ben in great detail.

"So you see, Ben, back in the 1970s, when the federal government started banned cigarette advertising on TV, and consumers started winning health lawsuits against the cigarette companies, the Synoid saw the writing on the wall, and they convinced the cigarette companies to diversify into the food industry. It was the perfect fit. The tobacco companies had all these advertising experts and chemists on their staff, so prepackaged food simply became the new tobacco. Philip Morris bought General Foods and Kraft Foods, and R.J. Reynolds bought Nabisco. I bet you didn't know that eighty percent of the world's processed food manufacturing is controlled by five tobacco companies. And those five tobacco companies are applying the same chemistry and strategies they used with cigarette to create and sell the processed food that you eat. You are probably too young to remember candy cigarettes, but back in the fifties, the cigarette companies gave away candy cigarettes to children in an attempt to indoctrinate children to the pleasures of smoking. The tobacco companies used the same techniques to market food. The tobacco companies bought up brands like Kool Aid, Hawaiian Punch, and Tang, and applied their flavor-enhancing experts and their marketing experts to get children addicted to sugary drinks. And they did the same with all their processed food—they added hyper-palatable chemicals to get people addicted to fast food and ultra-processed foods. Have you ever looked at the list of ingredients on a box of processed food? There are more chemicals than there are food ingredients. Why? Because if the Synoid can control what you eat, they can control what you think."

"But doctor," Ben said, "it's a big marketplace. There are places like Whole Foods that sell healthy foods, and there's lots more education available now about what is good food. People have a choice."

"Nah," said Dr. Gaye dismissively. "The Synoid is only giving you the illusion of free choice. There is no free choice. Look, there's a reason why heroin is illegal. If heroin was legal and you could buy it anywhere and smoke it or shoot it up anywhere, you know what would happen? Everyone would use heroin! Why? Because it feels too damn good! To say that it's okay to allow ultra-processed fast food because people have the freedom *not to buy it* ignores the fact that people have become addicted to its taste. It's called comfort food for a reason. The Synoid controls the advertising so that everything you hear or see proclaims that processed food is fun food. But once you try it, your body becomes addicted to it, and you can't stop using it. Do you know how many ingredients there are in McDonald's fries in the US? Nineteen. Nineteen! But in Europe, do you know how many ingredients they have? Three! Only three: potatoes, oil, and salt. Why the difference? Because the European Union won't let them add all those chemicals. There are so many chemicals used in US foods that are banned as unhealthy in other countries."

"So you're saying the US needs more food regulation?" Ben asked.

"Ha! That'll never happen. The Synoid controls the Congress and the FDA. Ninety-five percent of congressmen own stock in processed food companies. If congressmen start regulating food companies, all their stock portfolios would go down, and they don't want that."

"I thought all elected officials had to put their stocks in a blind trust," Ben said.

"That's a myth," Dr. Gaye said. "There is no such requirement, nor will there ever be. That's why things will never change. Why would a single elected official vote to do something that would hurt themselves? It's against human nature. Self-preservation and self-enrichment—those are the enduring principles. That's what makes the Synoid's control so easy. The Synoid doesn't have to lift a finger; they don't have to bribe anyone. They just let human nature take its course."

Dr. Gaye paused for a moment. A look of sadness came over his face. "You know, Ben, when I first invented Dopa, I had such high hopes of being able to help people. But then, when I met with the bankers at Goldman Sachs, and they told me how much money I stood to make... well, I became greedy. I got swept away with the idea of being fabulously wealthy. I was just like those idealistic congressmen when they first realize how much money they could make from all the insider information they learn in their secret hearings. I started off wanting to change the world and then I got seduced into wanting to rule the world..." Dr. Gaye shook his head. "What a waste, what a huge joke." He shrugged, looked at Ben, and said, "That's how the Synoid gets you, you know. They take you to the top of the mountain, show you the world, and just whisper in your ear, 'All this shall be yours if you worship me.' That's how it's done, Ben. And one hundred percent of people succumb. There's nothing like greed, Ben. Greed is a torrent that sweeps everything away."

Ben stopped writing and looked at the sadness in Dr. Gaye's face. "But you still have Dopa, Dr. Gaye. It's a breakthrough drug. It'll save thousands of lives."

Dr. Gaye gave a weak smile and shook his head no. "Dopa is flawed, Ben. That's the big joke. I was so eager to give Dopa to the world that I became an easy mark for the Synoid. They tricked me into selling my soul. Then the gods pulled the rug out from under me."

"But doctor, Dopa can cure addiction!" Ben exclaimed.

Dr. Gaye continued shaking his head. "No, Ben. Dopa only blocks addiction for a short while. And then Dopa begins to mutate, and the tyramines revert to phenethylamines, and then the amygdala starts to change."

"I don't understand," Ben said.

"Dopa is flawed," Dr. Gaye said in a flat voice. "It only works temporarily. I thought it would be a permanent cure for addiction, but it isn't. The body adapts and changes Dopa into something else."

Ben just stared at Dr. Gaye with a confused look.

"My best estimate, Ben, is that Dopa is only effective for five years. I thought it cured addiction permanently. But I was wrong. After about five years, it mutates. Or rather, the brain mutates. That's the big joke, Ben. Dopa isn't a cure. As soon as Stanford realizes that, they'll close the drug trials down. There will be no investment, no IPO, no FDA approval, no cure for addiction."

"I-I don't understand, doctor," Ben said. "If Dopa doesn't cure addiction, what does it do?"

"Well," Dr. Gaye smiled. "It *does* allow you to see the Synoid."

CHAPTER TWENTY-ONE: INTERLUDE

Reno, Nevada

Darryl was now up to using Dexedrine three times a day and taking diazepam at night to sleep. His job driving the mini-van for the casino was going well, but Darryl noticed that he was often jittery. He went to a doctor and got a prescription for Librium to calm his nerves while he drove. Of course, he didn't tell the doctor about the Dexedrine or the diazepam. He just said he was having anxiety on the job. The combination of the three drugs seemed to work. Darryl was making decent tips as a driver, and his time behind the wheel seemed to fly by. The only problem was there was always that thirty-minute wait at the casino between the time when he dropped off people from the airport, and the time he was scheduled to take the next group of hotel guests to the airport. The thirty-minute gap happened four times a day, and there was nothing to do but sit around the casino waiting for his next trip. That was the most boring part of his job. Occasionally, he would pass the time playing the penny slot machines. It was only thirty minutes, he told himself, and his maximum bet was only a nickel. He kept it under control.

* * *

San Francisco, California

Before the doctor discharged Steven from the Emergency Room, he tried to talk to him about rehab again.

"If keep using street drugs, you're going to die," the doctor said. "All of them are laced with fentanyl. We're getting thirty to forty overdoses a week in here. Every single one of them is fentanyl. I can have our social worker come and talk to you about getting into a rehab program. The State has programs that can get you off the street."

Steven just shook his head. "I've been through every rehab program in town," he said slowly. "None of them work."

"This is your fourth overdose this year, Steven" the doctor said. "If you keep using, you're going to die."

Steven had heard this talk before. Usually, he would just nod and say some bullshit about trying harder. But today he finally said out loud what he had always thought. He looked at the doctor and said, "I don't care."

*   *   *

Fort Lauderdale, Florida

One of Richard's friends at the bathhouse invited him to a 'party and play' event at a private house. These events were forty-eight-hour orgies fueled by methamphetamine. The experience was the most exhilarating, amazing experience Richard had ever had. He was completely hooked. He submerged himself into the subculture, making more and more contacts on the gay internet. Soon he was going to P&P events every weekend.

*   *   *

Charlotte, North Carolina

Madeline was able to get a second equity loan on the house she had inherited from her sister. That allowed her to pay those past-due bills and gave her some breathing room. She continued to go to the Indian casino every day and play the slot machines. And of course, she continued to buy the on-line lottery games. She knew she was going to win the big jackpot sooner or later.

* * *

Tulsa, Oklahoma

Martin sat in his jail cell. His life was over. He couldn't do three years—he just couldn't. How had he managed to fuck up his life so bad? He started to contemplate suicide. He would need to find some kind of rope, something he could use.

* * *

CHAPTER TWENTY-TWO

Villa Rosario, Panama

Dan had not seen his friend don Fernando for several days. When don Fernando called him and suggested lunch, Dan accepted immediately.

"Oh, Dani, we have much to talk about," don Fernando teased over the phone. "But I will tell you over lunch. Let's meet at Soda Linda at noon."

At Soda Linda, after they had ordered food, Dan asked, "So what's been going on?"

"So much, Dani. So much!" don Fernando said, and launched into his update. "Three days ago, I got a threatening email. It was just one sentence, and it said I should release the gringo or I and my men would be killed, and it was signed Sinaloa."

"Sinaloa?" said Dan. "Like the Mexican cartel?"

"Yes, Dani, the Mexican cartel. They are trying to infiltrate Panama, but we have our own gangs, you know. And so, there is much rivalry. But I will explain. So I get this email, and the only gringo I have in custody is the crazy doctor, so I knew they were referring to him. But I also know that the Sinaloa cartel does not send emails. So I gave the email to Carlos Wang, my computer expert. You remember him? He traced the IP address to a computer in La Chorrera. So Carlos sent them a bunch of phony emails, where we pretended we were going to turn over this Dr. Gaye to them in front of the Catholic Church in La Chorrera. Of course, we had undercover police stationed everywhere. And guess who shows up?"

"Who?" asked Dan.

"Two idiots on a motorcycle, Dani. And can you guess what motorcycle they were on?"

"The one with the license plate? The one that Dr. Gaye saw outside his hotel?"

"Yes, Dani!" don Fernando laughed. "That very same one. Two dumb wanna-be gangsters. They belong to a drug gang called Bagdad. This Bagdad group is big in Colón and Panama City. They handle a lot of the street-level drug sales *inside* Panama. And they are rivals with another group called Calor. The Calor group mainly handles distribution of drugs *through* Panama. So, the Calor gang sells drugs to the Bagdad gang. But they are also rivals, so sometimes they kill each other. It's a complicated, stupid business. Anyway, both gangs are trying to impress the Sinaloa cartel, because they both recognize that Sinaloa is eventually going to be the big kid in town. So they are both trying to align with Sinaloa, hoping Sinaloa will chose them to be their drug distributor inside Panama."

"This sounds fucked up, don Fernando," Dan said.

"Oh, it is, Dani. It is very fucked up! Panama is cursed by its location. Drugs either move through here overland into Costa Rica, or they move to our ports to be shipped to Europe, or they sail along our coast, stopping here for fuel and supplies. But anyway, we see these two punks on their motorcycle with the same license plate number that Dr. Gaye gave me. So, we stop them and search them. And well, well, they both have guns on them. So we arrest them. And then I have a little chat with them, if you know what I mean."

Dan Landes knew exactly what don Fernando meant when he said 'a little chat'. Don Fernando was an old-school police chief, meaning that he believed his highest duty was to uphold the law and protect the citizens under his domain by any means necessary. Even if that meant breaking the law to do so. Such methods ran directly counter to Dan's own training as a detective decades ago in Los Angeles. But Dan also knew that parts of Panama were like America's old west: wide-open territory full of outlaws. Don Fernando's methods were often the only law around.

"And what did you find out?" Dan asked.

"These two punks confessed to being members of the Bagdad gang, and they *had heard* that the Sinaloa cartel *had heard* rumors about Dr. Gaye's Dopa drug—you know, about how it was going to end drug addiction in the United States, and all. Well, you know how rumors are. It's true that the Sinaloa cartel always get nervous about anything that might interfere with their business. But it's unclear if they were planning to do anything about Dr. Gaye. They were probably just watching the situation. But these two punks decided that they would beat the Sinaloa cartel to the punch. They were going to impress the Sinaloa cartel by killing Dr. Gaye—you know, to show how ruthless and violent they were. But they were just low-level street gangsters, and they were really incapable of pulling off something like that. It's a shame to see young Panamanian boys so stupid and delusional about their place in the world."

"So, let me understand, don Fernando. They sent you an *email* to try and intimidate you into releasing Dr. Gaye so that they could kill him?" Dan asked in astonishment.

"Basically, yes, that's it," don Fernando said.

"And then you responded and said 'yes'... and they *just showed up*?

"Pretty crazy, huh?"

"That's insane," Dan said.

"I thought so too, Dani. These boys are from Colón. They are very stupid. They did not know how we do things around here."

"What are you going to do with them?"

"I've already shipped them to a high-security prison in Panama City. I convinced the prosecutor that they were cartel gang leaders planning a terrorist attack on a police station. Then I call Judge Cordela in Panama City—remember him? He's married to my wife's sister. Anyway, I asked him to authorized a year of pre-trial detention for these two boys. I told him I needed a year to investigate this *horrible crime*. Of course, there's nothing to investigate. These two boys were so scared after my little talk, that they confessed everything. But I wanted to get them out of the way for a while. And of course, Judge Cordela is family, and he hates stupid criminals as much as I do. So, he granted my request. Those boys will spend the next year in a horrible adult prison. That may not change *their* ways, but it will get them out of *my* way.

"But, you see, Dani, the problem is not these two punks, and the problem is not the Sinaloa cartel. The problem is that the world is full of dumb wannabe punks. And if the idea of killing Dr. Gaye occurred to these two idiots, it could easily occur to other idiots. So my real problem is Dr. Gaye. Obviously, it has leaked out that he is in our jail. So, two days ago, I had him relocated."

There was a little twinkle in don Fernando's eye. "Can you guess where I moved him to, Dani?"

Dan shook his head no.

"You might remember the place," don Fernando teased. "An old-fashioned villa at the top of the Cerro La Monita mountains... hard to get to, but a great view... plus he's under a doctor's care there..."

A sudden recollection came across Dan's face. "Not that crazy witch doctor?" Dan exclaimed.

"Yes," don Fernando said and smiled. "Dr. Emilio de la Cruz. One of my oldest and dearest friends. He graciously agreed to host Dr. Gaye for a week while I figure out what to do with him."

"That Cruz guy is no doctor!" Dan exclaimed. "He's a sadist."

Don Fernando laughed. "He cured *you*, didn't he?"

"He nearly killed me!"

Dan was correct when he said that Dr. Emilio de la Cruz was not a doctor. Technically, he was an herbologist, a collector of medicinal plants. 'Doctor' was a purely honorary title that the older residents of Villa Rosario had given him decades ago, before any medical clinics came to the town. But don Fernando was also correct when he pointed out that Dr. Cruz had cured Dan. For it was almost ten years ago, when Dan life was consumed with his devotion to—and daily use of—the psychedelic drug ayahuasca, that don Fernando had kidnapped Dan and taken him to Dr. Cruz's villa for a week. There, Dr. Cruz tricked Dan into drinking an herbal tea that began a week of vomiting and purging. It was a brutal, horrible week in Dan's life. But it did break his addiction to ayahuasca. Dan was grateful to have been given his life back, but he vowed never to speak to Dr. Cruz again.

"He's a madman," Dan exclaimed.

"Yes, but so is Dr. Gaye. So they will have much to talk about. But the point is, that Dr. Gaye will be safe up there. I released an announcement that we had deported him back to the States. This way, I won't have any other idiot gang members sending me emails or driving around on their stolen scooters."

"So, who knows that Dr. Gaye is up there?"

"Just you and me. Oh, and that reporter Ben what's-his-name. Dr. Gaye has grown quite fond of him. They talk all day long. And as you know, Dr. Cruz is very old, and I figured that he might need some help managing Dr. Gaye. So, I made a deal with the reporter. I told him what I was doing with Dr. Gaye, but he had to agree to also go stay at Dr. Cruz's villa and help Emilio take care of Dr. Gaye. I told him it would only be for a week."

"What happens after a week?" Dan asked.

"Well, I'm not sure yet. I'm debating just actually doing what I said. That is, just sending him back to the States. As far as I'm concerned, I have solved the question of who shot at him at his hotel. And by locking those two gang members up, I have removed the threat to tourists. My work is basically done."

"What about the counterfeit passport, don Fernando?"

"Ah Dani, I really don't care about that. It does not affect my town or La Chorrera."

"So, why wait a week?" Dan asked. "Why not just deport him right now?"

"Because something bothers me about this case, and I can't quite put my finger on it, so I wanted to let it... what is that word you gringos use? Percolate? I want to let it percolate for a few days. I want to see what comes up."

Dan nodded.

"The other thing that moving Dr. Gaye does for me," don Fernando continued, "is that it gets rid of that pesky little fat man from New York. He was so mad when I told him that Dr. Gaye had been deported. He stormed out of my office."

"That guy from the Synoid hedge fund?" Dan asked.

"Yes, Dani. He had gone with some lawyers to Panama City to try and get a guardianship issued so that he could take Dr. Gaye with him back to New York. But I asked Judge Cordela to block it. So the little fat man came back to try and sweet-talk me into releasing Dr. Gaye to him. That's when I told him it was too late—that I had deported Dr. Gaye back to the States. Ha! Gringos get so mad when things don't go their way. His face turned so red. I thought he was going to have a stroke."

CHAPTER TWENTY-THREE

Villa Rosario, Panama

Dr. Gaye was very pleased with his new living arrangements. He enjoyed being free of his jail cell. He loved sitting out on Dr. Cruz's veranda with his morning coffee and watching the sunrise. Dr. Cruz had a housekeeper and cook who prepared meals for Dr. Gaye and Ben. Dr. Gaye rarely saw his host except after dinner where they had discussions comparing different medical stories. He was amazed by Dr. Cruz's knowledge of the effects of different plants on the human brain. During the day, Dr Gaye would expound on his theories about the Synoid and Dopa to Ben who wrote down everything he said.

On this particular morning, Dr. Gaye and Ben were sitting in the living room.

"I had a very interesting chat with our host last night," Dr. Gaye was saying to Ben. "The local people consider him a shaman, you know. They come to him with all sorts of physical problems, and he mixes up various potions for them. He and I do not agree on drug addiction, but I find his views very stimulating."

"How so?" asked Ben. "I mean, in what ways do you differ on drug addiction?"

"Well, to me, drug addiction is purely a chemical reaction that creates a behavior change," Dr. Gaye explained. "You take a person who has never been exposed to opioids, and you give him opioids enough times to where, if you withhold the drug, he experiences anxiety. Then his brain has *already* begun to change—he's *pre-addicted*. And if that person's prefrontal cortex has made enough sympathetic nerve connections to the dopamine centers of the brain, such as the ventral tegmental area and the hypothalamus, then he *will* engage in compulsive behavior to find and take that opioid again. If that compulsive behavior is successful in re-creating the dopamine rush, then that behavior is solidified, and he is addicted. That's the definition of addiction: the patient engages in compulsive behavior to re-experience the effect of whatever drug or activity he is addicted to. To me, it's a simple cause-and-effect relationship. The drug creates a rush of dopamine; the dopamine creates anticipation for more; the prefrontal cortex responds and creates new nerve endings; the brain starts to plan how to repeat the experience; a new behavior is created; the new behavior successfully creates the dopamine rush again, and the person is addicted. It's a learned behavior, but it's an irresistible learned behavior. The brain is changed—the *actual brain tissue* is changed. It's like a muscle you develop in the gym that stays with you all your life. That's why, for example, drug addicts or alcoholics who go through rehab and train themselves to stop their compulsive behavior can be clean for years, even decades, and then suddenly something will trigger that muscle memory, and they will go right back to drinking or drugging with the same intensity as before—as if they had never stopped."

"And Dr. Cruz has a different view of addiction?" Ben asked.

"Oh my! He certainly does," responded Dr. Gaye. "He believes addiction is a part of the human experience—that human beings evolved *because of* addiction. He thinks addiction is necessary for the species to survive."

"Really?" said Ben. "How can that be?"

"Well, he makes an interesting argument. He says that the earliest archaeological records show that psychotropic plants were used in all ancient civilizations. And he's correct about that. It's common to find fossilized plants buried alongside human remains in the most ancient of burial grounds. Using X-ray spectrometry, scientists have been able to identify cocaine metabolites in ancient Inca mummies, and both cocaine and THC in Egyptian mummies. Even art on cave walls has representations of the use of plants for ceremonial purposes, so I agree with him on that. Drugs have always been with us. But he takes it a step further. He believes that the compulsive drive to recreate that dopamine experience was the rocket fuel that propelled us out of the stone age. He claims that as soon as man learned how to make fire and cook food, they started combining different plants to get high. And that drive to get high motivated primitive mankind to organize into tribes, to explore, to develop language, and to refine more and more different drugs. Without drugs, he claims, there was no motivation to do more than the bare minimum to get enough food to eat and procreate. He thinks that without the addiction to drugs, man's behavior would be no different than a dog: so long as there is a warm fire and something to eat, there is no motivation to move. But drug addiction forced mankind to evolve, in a constant search for more dopamine experiences."

"That's crazy," said Ben. "I've seen fentanyl addicts! They can't even move. There's no motivation there."

"That's only a recent development," said Dr. Gaye. "The whole refinement and industrialization that creates the super-drugs that we have today—that's all very recent. Mankind has never had such powerful drugs. The mountain people of the Andes have chewed coca leaves since the beginning of time—and their bodies have adapted to that addiction—but they never had to deal with crack cocaine, a million times more powerful. But when I pointed this fact out to our host, that it is the new scourge of super-drug addiction that I developed Dopa to fight, he asked me a question I could not answer. He asked me how I knew that Dopa wasn't just another part of the evolutionary process. He said that maybe it was no coincidence that I developed Dopa at the exact moment in history when the new super drugs became so addictive. He said that evolution is more than the physical changes that a species develops in response to its environment, but that evolution also includes the social and technological changes that a species develops. He suggested that the fact that Dopa allows an addict *to choose* whether or not to use drug may be some sort of evolutionary step."

Dr. Gaye paused. "Of course, I think our host is wrong about that, at least at the moment... maybe some reformulated Dopa... maybe in the future..." And Dr. Gaye's voice trailed off.

"You know," Ben said, "something you said back in the jail cell a few days ago confused me." Ben flipped through his notes. "You said that Dopa only works temporarily—you said, quote, that the body adapts and changes Dopa into something else, unquote. I didn't understand that. The Dopa trials at Stanford have been underway for almost a year. And according to the researcher I talked to there, the Dopa results are permanent—that as long as the patient takes Dopa, he doesn't have the craving to give into his addiction. He says that Dopa works well."

Dr. Gaye nodded his head up and down and exhaled. "Dopa works well," he repeated slowly, as if it was a question. "Well, that statement is true, in so far as it goes. But the problem, Ben, is that I'm not in the lab, so I can't test my new theory. But I *will* tell you my current thinking: addiction changes the brain. With addiction, the brain now knows what it's like to feel a huge dopamine rush. Every addict will tell you that there is nothing like that first time—that first time getting super high, or that first time winning a super jackpot, or that first time having super-taboo sex—there's nothing like it. And every addict always says the same thing—that while it was happening, they felt like *they were God*. Once they have that experience, then they are hooked. And then every addict spends the rest of his or her life chasing that first experience, wanting to recreate it, but it's never as good as the first time. But they *are* addicted—their brains have been changed, and they can't stop trying to get high again.

But then, we give them Dopa, and Dopa changes the brain again. Then suddenly the craving is gone, and the person can control their behavior. But they still have the memory of that dopamine rush, that powerful dopamine high. But Dopa is powerful, too. And now, the patient has a type of cognitive dissonance—they have the knowledge of what to have been God, but they also have super-rationality to know that there is no God. It's too much for the brain to handle. So then, I think the brain then makes a third change—on its own. I know I said that Dopa changes into something else, but what I meant is that it starts to have a different impact on the brain, because the brain itself has changed. I think that the brain is trying to synthesize the two types of knowledge, trying to reconcile the incredible power of being high, of being God, with the complete lack of craving ever to be God again. I think this conflict in the brain creates a new type of thinking... No, that's not right... it creates a new awareness of the world. And of course, that's what scares the Synoid. They don't want their customers having this new awareness. They want blind, obedient addicted consumers, not rational thinking humans."

Ben pursed his lips but said nothing. So many of his conversations with Dr. Gaye were like this. Dr. Gaye would start off sounding eloquent and completely rational, but then veer suddenly into a paranoid discussion of the Synoid.

CHAPTER TWENTY-FOUR: INTERLUDE

Reno, Nevada

Darryl was having difficulty finding sources for his Dexedrine habit. He couldn't find a regular doctor who would prescribe them. But he had a friend at the casino who introduced him to someone who had an in with a pharmaceutical company. That person was able to get legitimate Dexedrine from the factory. Darryl had tried some of the street level speed and didn't like it. But he trusted his new supplier. He knew that the drugs were being stolen from a pharmaceutical manufacturer, but that was not his problem. So long as he could get pharmacy-grade Dexedrine, he didn't care. He was now averaging four Dexedrine spansules a day. He upped his dose of Librium to twice a day to control the jitters, and he was still taking diazepam at night in order to sleep. Sometimes, after work, he would play a few rounds of Craps just to unwind.

* * *

San Francisco, California

This time, when the ambulance arrived at Steven's tent, they were too late. They gave him a shot of Naloxone directly into the muscle and administered CPR all the way to the hospital, but Steven was pronounced dead in the Emergency Room. He had no identification on him. The EMTs only knew him by his street name of

Cupcake, but the police found his California EBT card inside his tent that gave his real name. Eventually, by contacting all the rehab centers in the San Francisco area, the police were able to track down Steven's only next of kin—an uncle who lived in San Rafael. The uncle just shook his head when the police came to his door. "I knew this day would come," he told the police.

* * *

Fort Lauderdale, Florida

Richard's doctor had the horrible job of telling Richard that his last blood test had come back positive for HIV. Richard couldn't believe it. He broke down and started crying right there in the doctor's office. "But I take PrEP," he protested. The doctor had to explain that while PrEP is very effective against HIV, it's not 100% effective. When Richard told him about the P&P parties, the doctor explained that using meth and poppers interfered with PrEP and lowered a person's resistance. The doctor also explained that now Richard would have to take a combination of antiretroviral medicines for the rest of his life, to prevent the HIV infection from becoming AIDS. And the doctor also explained that under Florida law, Richard was required to tell potential sexual partners that he was HIV-positive. Richard nodded his head but knew that he would never do that. If it got out that he was HIV-positive, he would never be invited back to the P&P parties.

* * *

Charlotte, North Carolina

For the second month in a row, Madeline was unable to make the payment on her equity loans. She avoided answering her phone when the caller ID said it was the bank calling. She still had her Social Security check, and she used that to continue playing the online lottery games and to play the slot machines at the casino. If she could just hit one jackpot, she could get those bastards at the bank off her back.

* * *

Tulsa, Oklahoma

The jail placed Martin on suicide watch after his botched hanging attempt. He was stuck in a solitary cell in the hospital wing of the jail. Some guard was supposed to walk by his cell and check on him every fifteen minutes. There was nothing to do, no one to talk with. He started hearing voices. Martin felt that he was starting to lose his mind. After a month, he got one visit from the jail doctor who prescribed some type of drug. Whatever the drug was, it made Martin feel worse. So he pretended to take the drug, but held it under his tongue, and then spit it into the toilet after the guard left.

* * *

CHAPTER TWENTY-FIVE

Villa Rosario, Panama

Carlton Jimenez was not a happy man. His bosses at Synoid Capital had assured him that that fuck-wad Ron Glass would be able to negotiate the release of Dr. Gaye. That certainly the fuck had not happened. Ron Glass had returned to New York like a wet rat with his tail between his legs telling the bosses that Dr. Gaye had been deported. But Carlton Jimenez knew that wasn't true. Carlton had been keeping surveillance on that shit-hole police department since day one. He had seen the police escort Dr. Gaye out to an unmarked car and drive away. Carlton had followed that car up into the mountains. He knew that they were keeping Dr. Gaye under wraps for some fucking reason. And the very afternoon after they had transferred Dr. Gaye out of the jail, that fucking police chief had fucking lied to Ron Glass to his face and told him that Dr. Gaye had been deported! Something fucked-up was going on. Were these hick cops in cahoots with the DEA? The CIA? Or had they just figured out what Synoid Capital was up to? Fuck. Ron Glass had certainly screwed this job up. But of course, Carlton Jimenez had one advantage over Ron Glass: he spoke Spanish. Why his bosses had sent the non-Spanish-speaking Ron Glass down to Panama was a fucking mystery. It's a foreign country, for fuck's sake! Ron Glass stood out like a sore thumb with his white-white skin and his fat gringo body. But Carlton Jimenez knew how to blend in. He hadn't grown up in Mexico for nothing. Mexicans survive by blending in. It's part of the culture.

So now, Carlton had to figure out what the cops were up to, and more importantly, figure out a way to force Dr. Gaye to go to New York. If this was the States, it would be easy. He could just tap him on the head, wrap him in a blanket, throw him in the back of a van, and drive him to New York. But fuck, that would be impossible here. Plus, they had that gringo living in the house guarding Dr. Gaye. Carlton didn't know who this gringo was. He had shown up at the jail every day whenIzed Dr. Gaye was a prisoner there. The police all greeted him. But he wasn't a local. He had been staying in a hotel in Panama City. And Carlton noticed that he always carried a notebook with him wherever he went. He must be CIA, Carlton thought, sent here to debrief Dr. Gaye. How else could he have such easy access to the jail? Plus, this gringo clearly knew about the plan to move Dr. Gaye out of the jail, because he had checked out of his hotel in Panama City and had ridden in the same unmarked police car with Dr. Gaye up into the mountains, and hadn't left that mountain retreat since then. Fuck, he must be CIA. Which meant he would be heavily armed.

Carlton had made some discrete inquiries around Villa Rosario. He learned that this mountain house belonged to a local shaman, an old man who was known for selling magical cures. That was probably just local code for a drug dealer. So the cartel was in on this deal. But why would the police give Dr. Gaye to the cartel? Maybe they had no choice. Maybe the cartel simply demanded Dr. Gaye. But wait, why would the CIA go along with that? Unless... unless the CIA was working with the cartel. That made sense. Everyone knew that the CIA had been partners with the cartels since the days of Pablo Escobar. So of course, it all made sense. The CIA and the cartel had threatened the police into releasing Dr. Gaye to them, and they were keeping him in this mountain hideaway, probably torturing him, and extracting all sorts of information out of him. Fuck—if they killed him, the Dopa project would be sunk. Carlton had to think fast. He had to get Dr. Gaye out of that house and on a plane to New York before the CIA and the cartel killed him.

CHAPTER TWENTY-SIX

Villa Rosario, Panama

Dr. Emilio de la Cruz had been mixing potions and administering them to the locals for more than half a century. He was well into his eighties now, but still went out daily to the mountains above Villa Rosario to pick plants. The indigenous people of these hills did not trust the young doctors at the clinic down in Villa Rosario with their shiny faces and their pointed needles. Besides, none of the locals had cars, and it was a day's walk down the mountain to go to the clinics. But they knew and trusted Dr. Cruz, and they came to him for remedies for everything from stomach aches to cancer. Dr. Cruz had a small office in the front of his villa where he would see clients. For those too sick to travel, Dr. Cruz would go to them.

He treated almost every type of malady, but one of his specialties was treating addiction. Many of the young indigenous people of the area, like young people of all generations, had become disenchanted with the cultural ways of their parents. They all complained that life in the community was boring. So they took to fermenting sugar cane into an alcoholic brew called seco, and then, for added excitement, they mixed the seco with the crushed leaves of the chacruna plant, a small bush that grows in the mountains all through Central and South America. Those leaves contain small amounts of dimethyltryptamine, or DMT, a psychedelic alkaloid. This particular concoction of seco and DMT allowed the young people to get very high and drunk at the same time, causing them to stumble around the villages in a complete stupor, alleviating their boredom but sometimes causing their death. The leaves of the chacruna plant were also one of the main ingredients in the psychedelic potion of ayahuasca, which happened to be Dr. Cruz's area of expertise—or, to be more accurate: curing clients of their dependence on psychedelics such as ayahuasca was Dr. Cruz's area of expertise. He had developed a rather potent herbal tea that induced intense vomiting that lasted a week. Patients would stay in a spare bedroom of his villa and spend every waking hour vomiting. It was an arduous process. No food would stay down, so patients often lost ten or fifteen pounds during their stay. Dr. Cruz made sure to keep them hydrated during these purging treatments. Once a patient started the treatment, there was no turning back. The vomiting simply would not stop until it had run its course for a week. Dr. Cruz told his patients that the herbal tea was magical and would cure their addiction, but secretly he knew that there was something powerful in the intense experience of purging that burned a new memory into the brains of his patients, and gave his patients something vivid and real to focus on.

    He tried to explain his theory to Dr. Gaye one evening over dinner. "You see, Disraeli, people need something real to grasp, something on which to focus their minds. You know what the most horrible punishment in the world is? It's solitary confinement. You lock a man in a dark room for three days, and he will go mad. The brain craves a focus; it needs external stimulation to maintain sanity; it has evolved for the sole purpose of directing its attention *onto something*. That's why every culture has religion. The masters need a way to keep the servants obedient, and religion is perfect for that. Religion has vivid images to look at; it has pageantry; it has unsolvable mystery and meaning to occupy the brains of the servants. Religion is perfect for social control because it always has external stimuli to focus on. You throw in an annual ritual with ecstatic dance or psychedelics to give the people a taste of the divine, and the people will be hooked. Yes, the brain needs external stimulation. It is both the cause of our evolution and the fatal flaw of our evolution."

"Say more, Emelio," Dr. Gaye said. "What do you mean, both the cause and the fatal flaw?"

"As I was saying the other night, the need for constant stimulation drove us out of the trees. Once our hairy ancestors discovered fermented fruit and psychedelic plants, they had to have more. Addiction to the experience that these plants provided caused our primitive brains to develop. We had to figure out ways to get high again. We developed drawing, to tell other cavemen what plants to look for. We developed agriculture, to grow and harvest the plants. We developed cooking, to process the plants into drugs that we could consume. Addiction drove evolution! That said, as our brains grew and developed into addiction-feeding machines, they evolved further and further down a particular one-way street. Now look at the human being, this so-called pinnacle of evolution! What a lopsided, weak creature. We have evolved bigger brains. But to what end? All the human being today is capable of is feeding itself more and more addictions. I've been to Panama City. I've seen how the modern man lives. They have invented these cell phone devices that they stare at all day long because the screens provide constant stimulation. Alcohol consumption has never been higher. The food is filled with addictive chemicals. The streets are littered with the bodies of addicts. I read an article recently that said that the Panama City ambulances pick up fifteen overdoses a day! The cartels are bigger and more powerful than ever—and why? Because people demand drugs to feed their addiction. No government can stop the cartels, because no government can control man's addictions. Addictions caused us to evolve, but we have evolved down a dead-end street."

"So... you think mankind is doomed?" Dr. Gaye asked.

"All evolution is doomed," Dr. Cruz said with a smile. "You know, we scientists have forgotten the definition of evolution. It's survival based on random mutations. But that survival is only temporary. Ninety-nine percent of all the species that have ever lived are now extinct. That's probably five billion species... all extinct! And it doesn't matter what mutation gave them a temporary advantage. They may have evolved horns, or armor-plated skin, or fifty-foot wingspans, or whatever—now all extinct. So, what we call human intelligence, this evolution of addiction-seeking behavior, is just another temporary mutation. Completely random. Other animals don't have it. It's simply our moment, our tiny moment, in the endless history of random mutations that we call evolution. Humans will certainly eventually die out. And ironically, maybe the very thing that drove our evolution will kill us. Maybe, addiction will kill us. Are you familiar with the Greek myth of Cronus? The god that eats its own children? That's what addiction leads us to—we have become gods that eat our own children."

Dr. Gaye nodded his head slowly. "That is rather a pessimistic view, Emilio."

Dr. Cruz made a dismissive movement with his hand, as if he was brushing crumbs off his jacket. "No, no, Emilio, not at all. I'm just describing the point we have arrived at so far—the rearview mirror perspective, so to speak. We still have about five billion more years until our sun burns out. I'm sure human evolution has a few tricks up its sleeve. Everyone forgets that evolution is *random* mutations. And random mutations are, by definition, unpredictable. As I said last night, maybe your Dopa drug is another random mutation that will change our direction. But anyway, for the moment, we still have time. And since we have finished a lovely dinner, I have a bottle of a very interesting wine I would like to share with you. I've been saving it for a special occasion. It is a bottle of Carménère wine, from Chile. I think you will enjoy it."

CHAPTER TWENTY-SEVEN: INTERLUDE

Reno, Nevada

Most days after work, Darryl was too wired up from the Dexedrine to go straight home, so he began spending more and more time at the Craps table, just to unwind. And he began noticing patterns in the numbers that came up on the dice. He started making mental notes of how a seven would always come up on the second roll after a four was rolled, and how the dice would hit six points in a row after a three or an eleven rolled. Then some buddy told him about Fibonacci numbers—how this Italian mathematician in the thirteenth century proved that there is no such thing as random numbers, that all numbers follow certain patterns in nature. The more he researched this, the more he saw how true it was. And the more he watched the dice roll, the more patterns he saw. And if the dice numbers were *not* random, that meant that a betting system could be developed to take advantage of this. Darryl started watching YouTube videos on how to use the Fibonacci sequence to playing Craps. This was it, he thought. He could use the Fibonacci sequence of numbers to create a system to beat the Craps table. That would allow him to quit his lousy job as a bus driver. He started staying up late, taking Dexedrine, searching the internet for more videos on Fibonacci patterns, and working on a betting system for Craps.

* * *

San Francisco, California

Doodle had heard that Cupcake had OD'd and died in his tent. "Fuck," he thought. He had just fronted that punk with ten Pink Cocaine pills to sell. Maybe, he thought, he could go into Cupcake's tent and find them. When Doodle got to the street where Cupcake stayed, he discovered that the police had taken down Cupcake's tent. "Fuck it," he thought. "Now, I'll never get my investment back."

* * *

Fort Lauderdale, Florida

Despite Richard's efforts to conceal his condition, word got out that he was HIV positive. Even though his viral load was undetectable, he stopped getting invited to P&P parties. His only sexual outlet was going to the gay bathhouses. But even there, his old partners shunned him, and potential new partners quickly heard the rumors about him, and also avoided him. He started traveling to other cities, to find bathhouses where he wasn't known. It was getting harder and harder to find good sex. He started to think about going back to Bangkok. He had to pay for the sex there, but there was never any problem finding ladyboys or male prostitutes. And he had heard that it was easy to get meth there.

* * *

Charlotte, North Carolina

Madeline was shocked when she discovered that the contract she signed for her home equity loans allowed the bank to seize her checking account if she was in arrears for her loan payments. They had taken almost all of her latest Social Security check. She tried calling lawyers, but none of them would take her case without an upfront fee. She went to a different bank to try and open up a new checking account. She must have been on some sort of secret bank blacklist, because none of the new banks would open a checking account for her. How could she get her Social Security money if she didn't have a bank account? She tried calling Social Security but they just put her on hold. Thank God she still had her credit card. She realized that she was too stressed out to even think straight, so she did the only thing she knew to do that would help relax her: she went to the casino to play the slot machines.

* * *

Tulsa, Oklahoma

After a month on suicide watch, the jail released Martin back into the general population. He found some cords in one of the janitor's closets and fashioned a noose and hung himself inside the closet. It was four hours before the guards realized that he was missing. When they found him, it was too late.

* * *

CHAPTER TWENTY-EIGHT

Villa Rosario, Panama

Don Fernando had noticed the white van parked just down from Dr. Cruz's villa for two days in a row. Being a curious man, he decided to investigate. There was no one sitting in the front, but don Fernando noticed that there was a curtain behind the front seats that obscured the cargo part of the van. He also noticed that the rear windows were covered with a curtain. The van had one small heavily-tinted side window, and the van was parked so that this side window faced Dr. Cruz's villa.

Don Fernando walked around to the other side of the van, where there was a sliding door, and knocked. He heard some movement from inside the van. He waited, then knocked louder. The sliding door opened and there, facing don Fernando, was the crouched-down figure of Carlton Jimenez, with a very surprised look on his face.

Don Fernando had not seen this man before. Clearly, he was not a local. He was thin, wiry, and dark-complected, with a thin mustache. If don Fernando had to guess, he would have guessed that the man was Mexican. Don Fernando's instincts were usually very good, and he also was convinced that the man was up to no good.

The man, on the other hand, knew who don Fernando was. He had watched him escort Dr. Gaye out of the Villa Rosario police station and into a car that had come up to this very location several days ago. Carlton Jimenez did not understand how don Fernando had discovered him sitting inside this rented van, keeping watch on Dr. Cruz's villa. But he knew that he did not want to interact with this police chief. Carlton reached over and grabbed the interior handle to the sliding door and tried to shut it, as if that would solve the problem. It was an instinctual reaction, something a child might do when caught red-handed by his mother. Instinctual, but completely ineffective. Don Fernando stopped the door from sliding shut with a simple push of his left hand.

"I don't think so, amigo," don Fernando said, and reached into the van with his right hand and grabbed Carlton Jimenez by the collar and jerked him out of the van, and pushed him up against side of the van. He held Carlton tightly by the neck with his right hand and quickly patted him down with his left hand. Suddenly his hand stopped moving when it felt an object in Carlton's right front pocket. Don Fernando carefully pulled out a small gun from the pocket and looked at it. It was a Ruger LCP pocket pistol, small but lethal. He tightened his grip on Carlton's throat.

"So, amigo," don Fernando said in the most unfriendly way, "what are you doing here?"

"N-n-nothing," Carlton sputtered.

"It looks to me like you are doing *something*, amigo," don Fernando said, and spun Carlton around and shoved his face into the sidewall of the van.

"In fact, it looks to me like you are up to no good." Don Fernando slid the pistol into his own pocket, unhooked his handcuffs from his belt, pulled Carlton's arms around his back and slapped the cuffs on him. Then he reached into Carlton's rear pocket and removed his wallet.

"Sit down," he barked, and moved Carlton so that he was sitting on the floorboard of the van, just inside the open sliding door. Then he opened Carlton's wallet, took out the driver's license and looked at it.

"Carlton Domingo Jimenez, New York driver's license. You're a long way from New York, amigo."

He put the driver's license back in the wallet and started thumbing through the rest of the contents. "Lots of fancy credit cards..." he said aloud, and then he stopped and pulled out a business card and read it. "Synoid Capital... well, well, well... it says here that you are an *operations consultant*. That's an interesting job title, amigo. Do you have your passport on you?"

"It's... it's at the hotel," Carlton spit out.

Don Fernando looked over the top of Carlton's head and scanned the inside of the van. It was a low-roof van, impossible to stand up inside the van, but comfortable enough to sit and stare out of the tinted window. There was a large chair positioned to face the window. Empty candy wrappers were strewn on the floor. There was also a pair of binoculars on the floor. Don Fernando considered the situation. Here was *another* employee of Synoid Capital. That was strange. Don Fernando had gotten rid of Ron Glass. Who was this guy? Clearly, this hombre was into surveillance. He must have followed them up to Dr. Cruz's villa. That meant that he wasn't there to spy on Dr. Cruz—he was there to surveil Dr. Gaye. Interesting.

"So... amigo," don Fernando asked, "why are you watching Dr. Gaye?"

"I-I'm not. I just stopped here to rest," Carlton exclaimed.

The fact that this hombre didn't act surprised at Dr. Gaye's name answered don Fernando's question. He was doing surveillance on Dr. Gaye! While don Fernando had never believed Dr. Gaye's paranoid ramblings about the Synoid, he had to admit that it was very creepy to find a Synoid employee following and spying on the doctor. Don Fernando looked up and down the road. He wondered if this guy was alone.

"Well, señor Jimenez, you are under arrest for not carrying your passport on you as required by Panamanian law. And you are under arrest for possession of a gun, which is strictly prohibited here in Panama. And you are under arrest for felony stalking. We are going to go down to the station, to *have a little chat*."

Don Fernando pulled his cellphone from his pocket, called the desk sergeant at the police station, and ordered a police car and a tow truck.

This used to be such a quiet little town, don Fernando thought to himself. All these gringos with their crazy talk and their corporate money and their guns were very annoying. The sooner he could ship Dr. Gaye back to the States, the better.

CHAPTER TWENTY-NINE

Stanford University, Stanford, California

Roger Matton had finally gotten up the nerve to ask Alison McPherson out to dinner. He used the excuse that there had been a new development in the Dopa project that he wanted to talk with her about. And that was true—something had happened that confused him, and he did want to brainstorm with her about it. Alison was probably the best scientist that Roger knew, and he valued her opinion, but he also just wanted an excuse to ask her out. And so, after ordering appetizers and cocktails, he launched into his story.

"So, we got the latest MMPI scores back," he said, "and once again they showed a very slight increase in Scale Six..."

"So the trend continues," Alison interjected, "except that now you have *four* months of increase, which is one-third of the length of your clinical trial, which under Fudd's Law, makes it a statistically *significant* event."

"Right," said Roger, "but there's a new twist. After I saw the latest MMPI results, I had the computer center administer another test, called the Raton Paranoid Thoughts Survey, or R-PTS."

"That's a different test than the MMPI?" Alison asked.

"Completely different. The MMPI measures personality. It looks at ten different—but general—psychiatric syndromes, like depression or anxiety; and it only includes one scale on paranoid thinking. But the R-PTS is not a personality test. The R-PTS *only* focuses on paranoia, and it measures paranoia on nine scales such as distrust of others, conspiracy theories, and feelings of persecution, et cetera. It's a very precise test, much more detailed than the MMPI."

"And what did that test reveal?

"That the people who were taking the real Dopa medicine were *not* clinically paranoid! Under R-PTS diagnostic model, a patient has to have elevated scores on five of the nine scales to be diagnosed as paranoid. But the Dopa patients only had elevated scores on two of the scales. And elevated scores on only two scales is not considered psychiatrically sufficient to be diagnosed as paranoid. But here's where it gets interesting. All the Dopa clients—that is, all the clients receiving the real Dopa medicine and not the placebo—scored higher on the *same two scales,* and that fact *is* considered statistically significant."

"Which two scales?" Alison asked.

"Social Hypersensitivity and Ideas of Reference. Social Hypersensitivity is just what it implies: extreme awareness of social cues. And Ideas of Reference is when you think that random events are directly related to you, so you attach meaning or make connections to things that have nothing to do with you. So, Ideas of Reference and Social Hypersensitivity—just those two scales. But in all the other paranoia scales, the Dopa clients scored normal."

Alison nodded. "And so, the increased score in these two scales is what drove the MMPI scores up?"

"Exactly."

"Interesting. And what's your interpretation of that?"

"Well, I don't know," Roger admitted. "I mean, at first I thought it was good news. I thought that it meant we could announce that Dopa was safe to use, that there is no statistically significant chance that it can induce paranoid thinking. It's going to make it easier to apply for FDA approval. But my problem is that, if you take away the statistics, it's really quite a baffling result. I mean, I understand how a medicine could make you hypersensitive to social cues. A lot of medicines, for example, change the way a person hears, so that they perceive more high-pitched sounds, or they make you more alert—those kinds of things—which could contribute to being more sensitive to what's going around you on a social level. I get that. But the fact that Dopa lets you make connections—false connections, really—between random events... well, I'm not sure how that's happening on a chemical level or what it means. Obviously, the drug is somehow stimulating the prefrontal cortex, probably in the medial area of the prefrontal cortex. But *why* that's happening, or whether it's good or bad, or what it means in terms of long-term Dopa use... we just don't know."

"And when was this R-PTS test developed?" Alison asked.

"2008, and then it was revised in 2021."

"And are there any other tests that are more accurate?"

"Not really. The R-PTS is about the best test that there is."

Alison nodded. "Well, you know, in clinical trials, you always have two processes going on, two areas you have to watch. First, there's the change in the participants—that's the obvious focus. But there's a second area, which is the reliability of the measuring instrument. There is always the risk of getting a false result, because the method of measurement is not sensitive enough. For example, if you're trying out a new antibiotic to see if it reduces infection, but you only have a thermometer to measure with, then all you can measure is whether the patient's temperature goes up or down. And while temperature is one aspect of infection, there are many things that can cause a temperature spike or reduction besides the effect of an antibiotic. So the sophistication of the measuring device is critical to the quality of the test results. You get where I'm going with this? Here you have a relatively recent test—this R-PTS test. It's some kind of questionnaire, right? A self-reporting test, where patients have to rate themselves? Kind of a primitive way to access whether someone has paranoid thinking, don't you think? I mean, you're basically asking the patient if they have paranoid thoughts. But you're saying that it's the most advanced, most sensitive test we have. That's more of a comment on our lack of ability to understand and measure mental illness, don't you think? It seems to me that paranoid thinking is such a difficult thing to understand, much less measure. My understanding is that no one really knows what causes paranoia, right? And here you have a drug that *seems* to *maybe* increase one or two aspects associated with paranoia, but the only reason you know that is because the patient is telling you that, which may, in itself, be a symptom of paranoid thinking. It's like that old conundrum: if a paranoid person tells you he's feeling paranoid, is that proof that he's paranoid or is it proof that he's not paranoid because he's able to distinguish paranoid thinking?"

Roger frowned. "So you're saying..."

"I'm saying that maybe you just don't know. Maybe you have to accept that there are possible unknown side effects of Dopa that cannot be measured." And maybe the best you can say is that there are no statistically significant negative effects that can be measured using current measuring tools."

Roger nodded.

"When do the clinical trials wrap up?" Alison asked.

"In about a week. The final report will come out in about a month."

"And so the final report will say that the drug is a success?"

Roger nodded again. "Yup, that's what we all expect." He paused for a moment and then added. "And *that's* what I told that Robert Wesley guy. He called me again, bugging me. He had somehow heard that I had ordered more testing, but I reassured him that those test had eliminated any lingering concerns about psychological side effects, so he was happy to hear that."

Alison gave a little laugh. "Yes, the test eliminated any lingering *statistical* concerns," she said. "But you still have some doubts, I can tell."

"Well, it just worries me when I see outcomes that I don't understand."

CHAPTER THIRTY: INTERLUDE

Reno, Nevada

Darryl had perfected his new Fibonacci betting system for craps, and just in time. The hotel had fired him from his bus driving job because he had started yelling at one of the guests. But the guy deserved to be yelled at. Darryl had a schedule to keep, and that motherfucker was making him late with his four huge bags of luggage. (Who the fuck brings that much luggage to a casino hotel?) So Darryl had lost it and threatened to punch the guy out. The hotel fired him that same day. But Darryl considered it a sign from God, because now he would have his days free to spring his new betting system on the unsuspecting casino. He was going to clean them out!

* * *

Fort Lauderdale, Florida

Richard booked a flight to Bangkok. He planned to stay a month. He put the flight and the hotel all on his credit card, because he needed to save his cash for sex and meth. He didn't have enough money to buy a month's worth of antiretroviral medicine, but he figured he would worry about that later. Besides, he felt fine. He was looking forward to having unlimited P&P time.

* * *

Charlotte, North Carolina

The bank foreclosed on Madeline's house. She was homeless. A social worker from the city got her into a women's shelter downtown. Her Social Security money was still tied up in the house foreclosure. The days of playing the lottery and the slot machines were over. All Madeline had in the world were the three suitcases she had brought to the women's shelter. Luckily, she still saved those extra sleeping pills. There was nothing left for her.

* * *

CHAPTER THIRTY-ONE

Villa Rosario, Panama

Most people think that jailbreaks are meticulous events, involving careful planning over a long period of time and flawless execution. The fact is that most successful jail escapes are spontaneous events—a combination of coincidence, opportunity, luck, and brazen action. And so it was with Carlton Jimenez and his escape from the jail cell at the Villa Rosario police department. A police car had taken him down the mountain from Dr. Cruz's house to the police station, where the police chief had grilled him for an hour and then tossed him into a tiny cell with just a bed and a toilet. There appeared to be three cells in the police station. As far as Carlton could see, he was the only prisoner. He could tell that there were many police officers coming in and out of the station during that day. The cell he was in was just down the hall from the front lobby of the police station, and Carlton could hear doors opening and closing, the shuffling of feet, and the muffled sounds of conversation that drifted down the hallway from the lobby. But Carlton noticed that as night approached, there were less and less policemen. Finally, after midnight, he stopped hearing any noises from the front lobby. It seemed that there was only one guard on duty, and that man seemed to be doing double-duty manning the front desk. And so, sometime after three a.m., Carlton started groaning loudly, and then called out for help. The sole guard came down the hallway. Carlton was in his bunk, holding his stomach, claiming he was sick with food poisoning, and demanding loudly to go to the hospital. The guard shook his head, but said he would get some medicine for Carlton to take. He returned a few minutes later with some pink pills. But as soon as he opened the cell door, Carlton sprung from the bed, and slammed the guard's head against the steel bars of the cell wall, knocking him out. Carlton stole his gun and slipped out of the cell, making his way quickly down the hall. There was no one in the front lobby, and Carlton slipped out the front door and disappeared into the night.

The next afternoon, a weary don Fernando was relating these events to Dan Landes.

"Oh, it was a terrible thing, Dani. I felt so bad for my poor guard. Luckily, he was not hurt too badly. The doctor said he will be okay. And I have changed the work schedule. From now on, whenever we have a prisoner, we will have at least two police officers on duty for the third shift. I will not let this happen again."

"And who was this guy?" Dan asked.

"Another one of those damned Synoid employees. I thought I had gotten rid of them when I told that little fat man that we had deported Dr. Gaye, but I was wrong. This guy worked for them, too."

"Really?" said Dan.

"Yes, I found a business card on him when I arrested him. It said he was an *operations consultant* for Synoid—whatever that means. But when I had a little chat with him at the station, he admitted to being a long-term employee of this company. He said he was sent in case that little fat man failed to get Dr. Gaye released. I still do not understand what this company does or why they are so interested in Dr. Gaye."

"It's a hedge fund, don Fernando. They are investors. They like to invest money into projects that make a lot of money. Unfortunately, hedge funds have a reputation for being very ruthless."

"Doesn't your government regulate them?"

"No, don Fernando. They are private companies. They are not regulated."

"Well, they are very annoying, and they seem to attract a lot of bad people. Ever since we arrested this Dr. Gaye, we've had nothing but outsiders invading the peace and quiet of my little town. First, punks on motorcycles with guns; then, little fat men with suits; and finally, this second Synoid agent, also with a gun, who attacks my officer. It's too much. So, Dani, I have decided to solve this problem."

"Oh," said Dan. "What are you going to do?"

"I'm going to ship this Dr. Gaye back to your country. I had a talk with this reporter person—Ben what's-his-name—and he has agreed to escort Dr. Gaye back to California."

"Wait, what?" Dan sputtered. "What about his false passport?"

"I do not care about that," don Fernando replied. "In fact, I never even reported it to Migration. Dr. Gaye can use it to leave Panama and re-enter the United States, for all I care. It is of no concern to me. The only thing I care about is protecting Villa Rosario. This Synoid group seems very determined to get Dr. Gaye. I thought I had solved the problem by moving Dr. Gaye up to Emilio's villa, but I was wrong. They just sent another agent. And it occurred to me today that if that dirty little operations consultant had *not* escaped my jail, then this Synoid group would have just sent yet *another* agent to replace him. I do not have the resources to monitor every foreigner who swarms into my town like a hungry horsefly. It will just be easier if I remove the bait that is attracting them. If this Synoid company is determined to pursue Dr. Gaye, let them pursue him in your country. It is the easiest way to solve my problem. In fact, it is a good solution. Dr. Gaye can be reunited with his family. His university can have their doctor back. The Synoid group can do whatever it is doing and leave my town alone. Also, this Ben fellow is very excited to go with Dr. Gaye back to California. They have become fast friends. The only downside is that Dr. Mendoza will be sad to lose his patient. He was very interested to see how this Dopa medicine was affecting Dr. Gaye's paranoia. But... science will have to wait. I have a town to protect."

Dan nodded slowly. He knew don Fernando was fiercely protective of Villa Rosario. So, within the logic of that devotion, sending Dr. Gaye back to the States did make sense.

"Have you told Dr. Gaye that someone from Synoid was doing surveillance on him?"

"Oh God, no!" don Fernando said. "We're trying to cure his paranoia, not increase it. No, I did not tell Dr. Gaye or that Ben fellow. I will tell Dr. Cruz after his guests leave his house."

"And when do they leave?" Dan asked.

"First thing in the morning," don Fernando replied. "Then we all can relax."

"And this escaped prisoner? What about him?"

"Oh, we will catch him eventually. There is a warrant out for him. I have already notified the border patrol and the airport police. He will not be able to leave Panama without being caught."

Dan nodded again, but to himself he wondered how secure Panama's borders really were.

CHAPTER THIRTY-TWO

Villa Rosario, Panama

"Are you all packed?" Ben asked Dr. Gaye.

"Yes," smiled Dr. Gaye. "Can't wait. It will be good to be home again. This trip to Panama has been... well, it has been quite an adventure. But it will be good to be back at the University. There is so much to do. The whole Dopa project has to be completely revamped. Dopa has to be reformulated. We will have to do new clinical trials."

"I'm still unclear, Doctor. I mean, I know you've explained it to me, but I just can't get my head around it. What's wrong with the current Dopa? I mean, it works. It cures addiction, right? And the only downside is that addicts have to keep taking it for the rest of their lives, but that's true with a lot of drugs, right? People who take Ozempic to lose weight have to take it the rest of their lives or the weight comes back. How is that different from Dopa?"

Dr. Gaye looked serious. "If I can be blunt, Ben, the difference is that if you stop taking Ozempic, you just get fat. If you stop taking Dopa, you get crazy. I tried stopping Dopa—and it made me crazy. I didn't realize how bad it was until I tried to stop. I couldn't stop. I would have gone back to taking it, but being in that jail kept me from my supply. Dopa is addictive, and it's addictive in a far more dangerous way than just opioids. Stopping opioids just makes your body sick, but you can get through that sickness with time and treatment. Stopping Dopa makes your mind change, and it just gets worse with time, not better."

"And so... *you'll* have to take Dopa the rest of your life?" Ben asked.

Dr. Gaye took a deep breath and nodded. "I'll have to continue taking this version of Dopa. Part of my new research will be whether a new formulation of Dopa can be made that doesn't make you crazy. I still don't understand chemically how Dopa does this—how it changes the brain. That'll be part of the new research. There is so much I don't understand. But clearly, this current version of Dopa is too dangerous to be approved."

"That's a shame, doctor. Addiction is such a huge social problem," Ben said.

Dr. Gaye shook his head. "You can't replace one problem with another problem, Ben. Society always does that, and it never works. People always grasp for the temporary, quick solution. But it *always* backfires. Instead of the cities being filled with addicts, they would be filled with crazies. No, the current version of Dopa is a failure. It has to be reformulated! The world will have to wait for a better solution to addiction... The Synoid will have to wait."

Ben tensed up. He didn't want to get Dr. Gaye started on the Synoid again. He tried to change the subject. "Will the University let you restart the clinical trials?"

"They won't have a choice. If they try to say Dopa is a success, I'll spill the beans, and that will ruin their reputation as a research facility. Reputation is everything to these universities—that's what keeps the money rolling in. No, Stanford will have to let me reformulate Dopa and start new clinical trials... unless, of course, the Synoid gets to them first. There's no virtue that can't be overthrown if you throw enough money at it. And the Synoid knows how to throw money around. That's how they get things done, you know. Their dirty money has infiltrated almost all levels of government and education. There's really no more good government and quality scientific education. It's all being distorted by the Synoid. Once they got control of the media, it was all over. That's the first thing any dictatorship does, you know. They take control of the media. And especially now, in our so-called technological age, everyone is so addicted to their cell phones, to the constant stimuli of 24-hour news, so when the Synoid got control of the news, they had a direct 24-hour video propaganda feed straight into the minds of the masses. Uncontrolled endless propaganda. There is no getting away from it. The Synoid has perfected the art of mind control. And of course, since the Synoid is invisible, the masses never realize they've been totally hoodwinked. They control all the schools, all the banks, and all the politicians."

Ben couldn't stand it anymore. "Dr. Gaye," he said, "pardon my saying this, but all this talk about some evil Synoid group behind everything—well, it just seems so... so *paranoid*. I mean, you're a scientist! Does it make any sense that some super-organized evil group is behind every bad thing in the world? That's just bullshit! It's something out of some James Bond movie."

"Who said anything about them being organized? That's the one thing in mankind's favor—the fact that the Synoid is so *disorganized!* Their left hand never knows what their right hand is doing."

"But you just said that the Synoid controls all the banks and all the politicians!"

"That's not because they're organized," Dr. Gaye responded. "I never said they were organized. God! If they were organized, we'd all be dead. No, the Synoid is as stupid and disorganized as can be. But! It's their collective *effect* that is dangerous. A group doesn't have to be organized to be dangerous. Look, if you have a town of a thousand people, and ten of them are stupid, then those ten people have no impact on the town. But if half the town is stupid—five hundred people—then you reach a tipping point, and then you start having stupid people on school boards and on the town council. Then one of them runs for mayor, and the collective effect of so many stupid people will doom the town with bad decision-making, poor planning, embezzlement, and corruption. That's the Synoid! It's not an organized brain trust! Just the opposite. It's the collective effect of millions of stupid people! Back in the day, Ben, when I went to high school, we had to study Latin. Latin! Plus, French or Spanish. Plus English grammar. We had to read the classics. That's gone! There's no more Latin in school. Hell, these days when high school graduates enter college, they have to be taught *remedial* English. They can't write proper English and therefore they can't construct a proper thought in their heads."

Ben just stared at Dr. Gaye with his mouth open. "I thought, all along, you were saying that the Synoid was some kind of highly sophisticated, organized group," he said.

"Well, *all* life forms will organize themselves. Hell, even inorganic matter organizes itself. Quartz atoms will organize themselves by sharing electrons with other quartz atoms so they can bond together to form crystals. Basic cancer cells will communicate with, and then connect to, other cancer cells. But that doesn't make them intelligent. The fact that something is *organized* doesn't make it intelligent. In fact, the more basic and stupid the organism, the stronger the organized bond. So, is the Synoid organized? Sure. Stupidity always bonds with stupidity. So, yes, you could say that the Synoid is a highly organized group. But are they intelligent? Fuck, no! They are the dumbest, most inept, cluster of morons that exist in the world. But... there's so many of them... so many of them."

"So... so you're just saying that the Synoid is... just *stupid people*?" Ben stammered.

"Well, not exactly, Ben, but close. And by stupid, I mean they are *only interested in benefiting themselves*. You should never underestimate the collective power of stupid people, Ben. Individually, they are just annoying, but collectively, they are responsible for all the evil in the world."

CHAPTER THIRTY-THREE: INTERLUDE

Reno, Nevada

At first, Darryl's new Fibonacci betting system worked great. He spent twenty-four hours straight at the craps table, just winning money hand over fist. Because of the Dexedrine, he could just keep going. He was almost twenty thousand dollars ahead. But then... something went wrong. He started losing heavily. He increased his bets just like his system told him to, but he still kept losing. Time seemed to speed up as he bet more and more. Then suddenly... his money was gone. He was completely wiped out. He stood up and stumbled from the table in a daze.

* * *

Fort Lauderdale, Florida

Richard's first week in Bangkok was going great. He found a connection for meth. He couldn't believe how inexpensive drugs were. Now he could party with the ladyboys and the male prostitutes all night long. He was in fucking heaven. But then it all came crashing down. The police came to his hotel room on a noise complaint and saw the meth on the table. The ladyboys all ratted him out. The cops put him in cuffs and hauled him away.

* * *

Charlotte, North Carolina

Madeline waited until everyone was asleep. Then she took all the sleeping pills she had and lay back down on her cot in the women's shelter. Her stomach began to ache, but a thick sense of fog seemed to envelop her. She had a dream where she was back in the Indian casino, just sitting at a clean slot machine. She was feeding dollars in and watching the wheels spin. She was happy.

* * *

CHAPTER THIRTY-FOUR

Oakville, California

It took some research, but Carlton had figured out where Lenore Gaye lived and had staked out her house. He wanted to get a sense of her routine, whether she worked, when she left the house, etc. He was pissed to discover she had kids. That always made kidnapping complicated. He couldn't have any witnesses.

It had been so easy to get out of Panama. Things are always easy if you have money, or are connected to money. That idiot guard had left his cellphone on his desk in the lobby, so Carlton had grabbed it as he left the police station. He only had to make one call to New York before he threw the phone away. Synoid Capital sprung into action and put Pedro Castanada on the next flight down to Panama. Pedro brought cash and a new passport for Carlton, and the two of them caught a flight out of Panama that night. Easy-peasy.

Carlton had worked with Pedro Castanada before. He liked Pedro. Pedro was Mexican, like Carlton, so that naturally made it easier. Plus, Pedro was a man of action. Pedro was one of those men who believed that the shortest distance between two points was a simple direct intimidating line. If there was something that needed delicate planning, Pedro wasn't your man; but if there was something that required immediate brute action, Pedro was the perfect person.

Carlton believed that his plan to kidnap Lenore made sense. For some reason, the police in Villa Rosario had released Dr. Gaye. Carlton didn't know why. Maybe that fat fuck Ron

Glass had somehow persuaded them after all, because the cops were just going to let him go. Typical Central American justice! They were always too lazy to prosecute anyone. So it stood to reason that if the police released Dr Gaye, he would probably return to California. And if Carlton was wrong in his assumption... if Dr. Gaye decided *not* to head straight back to California, then kidnapping his daughter would be just the thing to get him to change his mind and come home. It was the perfect plan. All he had to do was wait and see if Dr. Gaye appeared or not. Then he would act.

So, Carlton and Pedro took turns watching Lenore's house, keeping careful notes of her comings and goings. They rented a pick-up truck and filled the back with old lawnmowers, rakes, and weed eaters that they bought at garage sales. Both he and Pedro wore old gardening clothes and straw hats. In this neighborhood, nobody would notice a Mexican gardener with his truck of landscaping tools. Everyone would just assume they were working on some rich person's yard in the neighborhood.

Carlton kept in touch with his bosses in New York. He promised them that he would deliver Dr. Gaye to them. He didn't explain how, and they didn't ask. That was one nice thing about working for Synoid Capital, Carlton thought—they never asked too many questions.

Meanwhile, Lenore was going about her daily routine, but making a special effort to get her house cleaned up. She had received a call from Ben. He was bringing her father home to her! Ben explained that the Panamanian police were not going to charge Dr. Gaye with any crime. Lenore was so relieved. Ben put her father on the line and they talked for a long while. He sounded so much better than when she had talked to him in that jail weeks earlier. She was very excited.

CHAPTER THIRTY-FIVE

Copa Airlines had a seven-hour non-stop flight from Panama City to San Francisco. With the money that Ben had brought Dr. Gaye from his daughter, Dr. Gaye was able to buy two business class tickets, one for him and one for Ben. Ben insisted that he could ride coach, but Dr. Gaye said no. He would pay for the tickets, and Ben would ride with him. On the flight, Ben worked on his notes and peppered Dr. Gaye with questions to fill in the missing pieces.

"So, your plan is to reformulate Dopa when you get back to Stanford?" Ben asked.

"Yes, Ben. Dopa has to be completely redesigned. We can't release it the way it is—it's not safe. The FDA would never approve a drug to cure addiction that in itself is addictive. That makes no sense."

"And exactly how is it addictive?"

"That part I don't quite understand yet, Ben. It doesn't have anything to do with dopamine release—I know that. So, it must somehow alter the prefrontal cortex's relationship with the hippocampus. That's the part of the brain that makes connections between memory and understanding. My current thinking is that, somehow, Dopa alters that relationship. So, when a person stops taking Dopa, it disrupts his ability to convert short-term memory into long-term memory, which in turn disrupts his ability to make sense out of short-term memory. And he becomes paranoid. Somehow, the prefrontal cortex knows that Dopa is necessary to restore this balance, so it creates a craving to take Dopa again, you see—to restore this balance. It's a whole different type of addiction than dopamine addiction. Dopamine addiction makes you want to take a drug to feel good. Prefrontal cortex addiction makes you want to take a drug so you don't feel bad. But anyway... we are going to have to go back to square one on this Dopa project. We have to figure out a way to reformulate Dopa so that a person can stop taking it if they want and not feel paranoid. This is going to cause a huge delay. I estimate that it will take us a year to reformulate Dopa and another year to test it... so, we're at least two years away from releasing a workable Dopa to the marketplace. That's a shame. Addiction will kill a lot of people in those two years. And it's going to confuse the hell out of the Synoid. You see, Ben, one arm of the Synoid wants to stop us from releasing Dopa, so that group will be glad we are delayed. They don't want anything to interfere with their business model of selling addiction to the masses, whether it's in the form of sedatives, tranquillizers, casinos, pornography, or breakfast cereal. The whole American economy is based on selling addiction! So that arm of the Synoid will be overjoyed that we have to delay Dopa. But the other arm of the Synoid—the investment banks and hedge funds—will be furious with the delay. That arm of the Synoid sees the huge profit they can make off of Dopa. They are counting on that, so they will be trying to stop the delay. They will send agents to Stanford to try to get the university to release Dopa in its current form, so that they can get it to market as soon as possible. It's going to be a mess, Ben. No matter what we do, the Synoid is going to be behind the scenes, trying to influence us... either trying to stop us from releasing Dopa, or stop us from delaying Dopa."

Ben shook his head. "It just makes me crazy, doctor. How you can talk about Dopa making you paranoid in one breath and then talk about the Synoid working behind the scenes to interfere with you in the next breath?"

Dr. Gaye smiled and reached over and patted Ben's arm. "I understand. But believe me, the Synoid is real. You'll understand that when you get to my age. The Synoid is everywhere, always trying to gain control of your thinking. That's their whole methodology, you know... mind control. They want to control your mind so that you stop thinking, and stop trying to achieve your potential. They just want you obedient and compliant. Mass consumers—that's all the Synoid wants."

"But doctor, how do you know... well, how do you know that your understanding of the Synoid isn't being, um, created by Dopa?"

"Well, Ben, there's bad paranoia and then there's good paranoia. That's the part of the Dopa formula we need to keep. In a way, you're correct. Dopa does allow you to see the Synoid. But that's real! But a person who sees the Synoid when others don't, well, they sound crazy, don't they? The problem with Dopa is that when you *stop* taking it, it makes you *really* crazy. So the challenge for us is to *keep* the part of the Dopa formula that allows you to see the Synoid, and *get rid of* the part of Dopa that makes it addictive—the part that makes you paranoid when you stop taking it. It's a real challenge."

Ben didn't know what to say. "And the Synoid? What will you do about them?"

Dr. Gaye shrugged. "Duck and dodge, and keep moving. That's all you can do. It's always been that way. When Thomas Jefferson said, 'Eternal vigilance is the price of liberty,' he was talking about the Synoid."

"Really?"

"Oh yes. "The Synoid's been around since the beginning of time."

CHAPTER THIRTY-SIX: INTERLUDE

Reno, Nevada

Darryl stumbled into the men's room of the casino, went into one of the stalls, closed the door, sat down on the toilet and leaned against the wall. He felt he was in some horrible nightmare. He couldn't believe it. Now he was totally fucked. He had the shakes bad and no money left to buy more Dexedrine. He had lost all his money to the craps table. How? How did this happen to him again? He had a good job and he had fucked that up. He had saved some money, and now he was completely broke. He had beaten his gambling addiction for two years, and now all that was down the toilet. There was nothing left. He decided there was only one option. He had to act fast before the Dexedrine shakes made it impossible to walk. He stood up, managed to walk out of the bathroom and took the elevator up to the top floor. There he found the stairway that led to the roof. The sky was pitch black and the night air was cold. He had to act fast before he lost his nerve. He staggered to the ledge of the building, closed his eyes and took a deep breath, and then simply stepped off into the blackness.

* * *

Bangkok, Thailand

Richard couldn't believe it when they told him what the penalty was for first time possession of meth in Thailand.

Ten years in prison. Someone from the US Embassy came to visit him, but basically told him there was nothing they could do. The court proceedings were all in the Thai language. Richard had no idea what was happening. He didn't even know that he had already been sentenced until the guards took him to the prison. He was crammed in a tiny cell with ten other men, all Thai, no English spoken. He had to sleep on the floor. Cockroaches were everywhere. Only rice to eat. No showers. He got beaten up regularly. He tried to tell them that he needed his HIV medicine, but no one would listen. His life was over. Richard knew he was going to die there. It was just a question of when and how horrible it would be.

* * *

CHAPTER THIRTY-SEVEN

Oakville, California

Carlton Jimenez couldn't believe his eyes. He was sitting in the pickup truck talking to Pedro when a taxi pulled up to Lenore's house. Out stepped Dr. Gaye and the same young man that Carlton had seen going in and out of the police station in Villa Rosario. What a lucky break! Dr. Gaye had returned to visit his daughter just like Carlton had predicted. He pointed them out to Pedro.

"That's them!" Carlton said excitedly. "The older man is Dr. Gaye. The younger one is some gringo who was with him in Panama."

"Let's grab them now!" Pedro exclaimed.

"No, no, let's wait. See, they don't have any luggage. They must be staying at a local hotel or maybe at Dr. Gaye's house in Napa. They are just here to visit the daughter. Let's wait a few hours. They will have to leave at some point, and it will be dark soon. We can grab Dr. Gaye then. It'll be better."

"Okay," said Pedro.

Carlton turned his head and looked back at the bed of the pickup. "In fact," he said, "we need to go rent a van. We've got time. They'll probably visit for at least an hour. C'mon. Let's go downtown to that U-Haul store and get a van."

"Okay," said Pedro.

And so it was, that an hour later, a white U-Haul van pulled up and parked in front of Lenore's house. Carlton and Pedro sat inside the van and waited. Carlton had wanted to rent a plain white van, but the only vans that the U-Haul store had were clearly marked "U-Haul" along with a large green $19.95 painted on the side. Carlton rented the van anyway. He figured that his using a fake name and counterfeit identification would be enough to conceal his identity. He hadn't seen the surveillance cameras at the U-Haul store, and he certainly wasn't aware that Lenore had surveillance cameras on her porch facing the street. The police later used the videos from these cameras to piece together what transpired that night in front of Lenore's house.

About an hour after the van parked, the video showed Lenore, Ben, and Dr. Gaye exiting the house. A taxicab pulled up and parked in front of the U-Haul truck. Lenore hugged her father and Ben goodbye, and then stood on the porch and waved as the two men walked toward the waiting cab. As they got to the sidewalk, the video showed two men dressed as gardeners getting out of the white van. They both had guns drawn. Ben later told the police that neither men said anything. They just sprinted towards them and grabbed Dr. Gaye. But Dr. Gaye was nimbler than his age suggested, and he immediately punched the man closest to him in the face, and that man fell backwards to the ground. The other gardener then fired his gun at Dr. Gaye, and Dr. Gaye fell to the ground. On the video, Ben is then seen grabbing the gun from this second man. There was a brief struggle, but the video clearly showed Ben pulling the gun out of the man's hand and then stepping backwards and pointing the gun at the man. At that point, this second man turned and ran away. Meanwhile, the first man, whom Dr. Gaye had struck with his fist, got up halfway from the ground and pointed his gun at Ben and fired. That bullet missed, and police later found the slug imbedded in the wall of Lenore's house. Ben then fired his gun, and the man fell back to the ground. The video then shows the taxicab pulling away from the curb and speeding away. At that same moment, Lenore runs from the porch and kneels by her father. Ben is then seen pulling a cell phone from his pocket and dialing and speaking. The police later said this was Ben's call to 911. Then Ben also kneeled by Dr. Gaye and is seen on the video talking to Dr. Gaye.

The police arrived almost immediately. One officer spotted a man dressed in gardener's clothes running from the scene and tackled him. That man was later identified as Pedro Castanada. The other gardener was dead at the scene. His wallet contained three different driver's licenses under different names, but the police were eventually able to identify him as Carlton Jimenez. According to a business card in his wallet, Carlton worked for a hedge fund named Synoid Capital, but when contacted, Synoid Capital denied any knowledge of this man and claimed the business card was a fake. Dr. Gaye was taken to the hospital but died on the operating table. The surviving gardener, Pedro Castanada, denied knowing any of the parties. He claimed that the other gardener gave him the gun and forced him to go along with attempted abduction.

When later interviewed by the police, Ben's account of the events corresponded to what appeared on the video. He said that the two men suddenly appeared from the white van, holding guns. After Dr. Gaye knocked the first man to the ground, and the second man shot Dr. Gaye, Ben said he was panic-stricken and thought the men were going to kill them both, so he grabbed the gun out of the man's hand. It all had happened so fast that he didn't have time to think. He had no experience with guns and wasn't intending to shoot anyone, but when the man on the ground shot at him, Ben just pulled the trigger of his gun automatically. Lenore Gaye was too upset at the death of her father to be interviewed. The taxicab was stopped a few blocks from the scene. The car driver said he saw his customers being shot and thought it was a robbery and just wanted to get away as fast as possible. The police told Ben that they believed that the two men were trying to kidnap Dr. Gaye. The police theorized that they must have tried to kidnap him months earlier, and that's why Dr. Gaye had fled the country. That was their theory at least, and that was good enough for them to close their investigation.

EPILOGUE

Alexandria, Virginia

Three weeks later, Ben was back home in his condo in Virginia. His doctor had renewed his Xanax prescription and had given him two other medications to help him sleep at night. He still had not gotten over the events of three weeks earlier. His mind kept replaying the memory of that night over and over, as if it was trying to convince him that it really happened. He knew it all had happened, but he still couldn't believe it. Dr. Gaye was dead. And Ben had killed one of the attackers. Ben had never fired a pistol in his life, yet here he had shot a man and killed him. It just didn't seem real.

That night, as Ben knelt beside Dr. Gaye. Lenore was screaming and crying. Dr. Gaye's chest was soaked in blood. Ben heard police and ambulance sirens. Dr. Gaye reached up with one hand, grabbed Ben's shoulder and said, "Dopa...make sure Dopa gets out!" Then the ambulance medics pulled him and Lenore aside and started to attend to Dr. Gaye. The rest of that night was a blur.

Even after three weeks, Ben still had no idea what Dr. Gaye actually meant when he had said 'make sure Dopa gets out.' Did he mean to make sure that Dopa got approved *now*, or make sure that Dopa got reformulated and then released? Ben just didn't know. Before he flew back to Virginia, Ben had had several meeting with Roger Matton at Stanford and had told Roger everything that Dr. Gaye had said about Dopa being addictive and making people paranoid. Stanford had stopped the Dopa clinic trials and was closely monitoring all of the participants. Roger couldn't predict the future of Dopa but promised he would keep Ben informed.

Lenore was heartbroken. The shock of seeing her father murdered was more than she could bear, and she ended up being hospitalized overnight because of the trauma. Ben had stayed in California for a week to make sure she was okay.

Ben's girlfriend Sarah had been an indispensable help when Ben returned home. In fact, Ben didn't think he would have survived the ordeal if it hadn't been for Sarah's support. She helped him get into therapy, and she provided a sense of home and routine that seemed to ground him. He started thinking about asking her to marry him. He couldn't imagine living life without her.

ProPublica was also understanding and extended his deadline. Ben wanted to write something that was worthy of Dr. Gaye's legacy, that would both honor him and make sense out of what the last few months of his life had really meant. But every time Ben sat down at his computer to write, he struggled with how to properly describe Dr. Gaye, especially the last few weeks of his life. To Ben, Dr. Gaye's incoherent warnings about the Synoid and their sinister plots seemed like paranoid ramblings. Yet, somehow, when the police told him that the man he had killed was carrying a business card that said he was an employee of Synoid Capital, Ben wasn't surprised. In fact, it worried him that he *hadn't been* surprised. Was he starting to subconsciously believe Dr. Gaye's stories?

Every morning, Ben sat down at his computer with all his carefully organized notes, and tried to write a piece that accurately explained the complexity of addiction—a piece that described the horrors and tragedy of addiction, but that also conveyed how intertwined drugs were with mankind's evolution; a piece that laid out the chemistry of addiction, yet accounted for free will; a piece that depicted how addictive new street drugs had become, but that also indicated that new technology was just as addictive; and finally, a piece that conveyed how man's primitive brain simply isn't capable of keeping up with the new super-drugs and new technology... but every morning ended in frustration for Ben. It was all too complex, too intertwined, and evolving too fast. Ben knew that every good piece of reporting had to have a viewpoint, had to take a position, had to present some type of conclusion... but the problem was that Ben hadn't come to his own conclusion yet. Maybe the story had become too personalized. Maybe he was too wrapped up in Dr. Gaye's claim that Dopa made it possible to see the Synoid. Maybe he couldn't separate himself from the fact that he had killed a man from a company called Synoid who was trying to kidnap Dr. Gaye. None of it really made sense to Ben, so how could he write a story about it that conveyed a viewpoint, that conveyed a conclusion? There was no conclusion, at least none that Ben could find.

Finally, one morning, out of frustration, Ben simply decided to write the story chronologically, from start to finish, and let whoever read it draw their own conclusions.

And so... that's what he did.

-FIN-

ABOUT THE AUTHOR

Robert Rahula was born in Spain to an American father and Spanish mother but grew up in Virginia on the farm of his paternal grandparents. He returned to Menorca, Spain in the 1960s to pursue his writing career. Over the past thirty years, Robert has published dozens of books of prose and poetry in Spain and in the United States. Readings of his poems appear on his YouTube channel, his Facebook page, and his website robertrahula.com. He travels Europe and Central and South America for several months a year, giving readings and lectures, and spends the rest of his time writing.

www.ingramcontent.com/pod-product-compliance
Lightning Source LLC
LaVergne TN
LVHW010210070526
838199LV00062B/4524